the last
MADAM

A Legend of
the Texas Chicken Ranch

Joy Jones

TREATY OAK PUBLISHERS

ALSO BY JOY JONES

PUBLISHER'S NOTE

This is a work of historical fiction. Some of the characters, business establishments, and events are based on actual people, both living and dead, and their lives or circumstances, as recorded in public open records. All other material, including minor characters, dialogue, and events, is a product of the author's imagination. Other than the historical persons, any resemblance to actual people, businesses, or places is just a coincidence and purely unintentional.

Copyright © 2016 by Joy Jones

Cover photo of Chicken Ranch is courtesy of
Fayette Heritage Museum & Archives, La Grange, Texas.

Cover design by Kim Greyer

Permission to reprint articles in whole or in part has been granted by the following:

Robbie E. Davis-Floyd, *Journal of American Folklore*
Rev. Dr. Bernardo Monserrat, Center for Spiritual Living
Al Reinert, *Texas Monthly*
Forrest Wilder, *Texas Observer*

Printed and published in the United States of America

TREATY OAK PUBLISHERS
ISBN-13: 978-1-943658-06-0
ISBN-10: 1-943658-06-4

DEDICATION

This book is lovingly dedicated to my husband, James Nelson. His steadfast support, his contributions to the research and writing of it, and his devotion to me is my cherished treasure.

Praise for

THE LAST MADAM

The Last Madam, A Legend of the Texas Chicken Ranch is the scintillating story of one of Texas' most provocative, certainly one of the state's most colorful characters, of the 20th century. In this fast moving novel, The *Last Madam* simply has no slow moving parts. It gyrates from the get-go and leaves the reader with more than a mere glimpse into the shady past of the world's oldest profession. The bottom line is that with Joy Jones' meticulous research into the events of the times and the snappy dialogue of the characters, *The Last Madam, A Legend of the Texas Chicken Ranch* is just the beginning for this entertaining novelist."

Mary Elizabeth Goldman
Bestselling Author of *To Love and Die in Dallas*

To Texans, just the mention of "The Chicken Ranch" brings stifled chuckles, knowing quirks of the mouth, a forever acknowledgment of its place in our folklore. Reporters and writers, musicals, songs and a movie have defined much of what we think of the decades-old brothel in La Grange, shut down in the glare of a television lens in 1973.

Joy Jones has taken a different approach. Billed as historical fiction, her book is a look into the heart and mind of Miss Edna, *The Last Madam, A Legend of the Texas Chicken Ranch.*

From the young girl survivor of the Dust Bowl era through World War II, the prostitute in the seediness of Post Office Street in Galveston, to the bawdyhouse businesswoman in

La Grange, we experience Edna Milton's evolution as a woman, as a person.

The surprise of the book is the continued journey of Milton, and what we find is a new account of the world's oldest profession... after the legend died.

Shara Fryer
Former lead anchor, Channel 13, Houston, TX

the last MADAM

A Legend of the Texas Chicken Ranch

FAMILY DAMAGE

The past is not dead, it's not even past.

William Faulkner

In an instant, everything changed—I can still hear the complaining old bed in that shadowy attic, but I didn't get past 'what's happening?' Those hot, hurried moments persist in my memory, even now.

Yes, decades later, I can still see that old ranch house in my mind's eye. At the time, I didn't understand it was the ranch manager's house. All I knew was that it looked grand to me, and I took pride that my relatives lived there. It stood solitary and unadorned on the flat Oklahoma prairie. The 'needing to be painted again' white fence surrounding it didn't distinguish the yard much at all from the pasture for the cows. No rose bushes or shade trees or happy flowers in the unwatered yard.

And I knew we wouldn't be going in the door facing the dirt road. The front porch was small and unused, and the door seldom opened. All the family reunion fun I looked forward to every year was in and out the side door.

I suspect the house didn't feel the same way. The annual Milton family gathering was noisy and Uncle Ken and Aunt Jean's two-story, large frame house shuddered with the young kids running in and out the slamming screen door.

My grandma insisted the family get together once a year, and I was grateful for her decree. As long as I could remember, we moved around from pillar to post, as Mother put it, for Dad to find work. Mostly he sharecropped, but not always. Sometimes he tried his hand at working as a mechanic at a filling station. Mother just had kids and worried aloud about never having enough money.

I can remember living in an attic once where Dad could only stand up straight right down the middle of the one long room. But the rental in the alley was the worst. Two rooms with only a pigtrail between beds. However, the mental effects rather than the physical have followed me all my life. That mantra of Mother's must have gotten into my DNA because how else can I explain my fear of not-enough-money.

Even now, decades later, I can get an anxiety attack just walking into a bank. I haven't been able to rid myself of the feeling that regardless of what my bank statement shows, there just might not be enough money to last me. Shit! What nonsense, but I'm afraid this certainty will, like as not, follow me to my grave.

But, at the age of eight, riding in the back seat of our old Ford car, I didn't have money worries. All I knew was we didn't have enough, but today I would get to play with my many cousins and ride horses, under Uncle Ken's supervision. That was enough to make my heart sing.

And I might be the last one out of the back seat, but I was the first one to swing open the screen door. The large screened-in porch was already filled with fat aunts shelling peas and shucking corn, and delicious kitchen smells drew me farther into the cool, dark house, and into Aunt Jean's apron and her warm arms. This I could count on. Every year... the same house, the same food, the same people, and the same horses, with my favorite uncle eager to help us kids ride.

When I was living it, I didn't realize this reunion weekend was the only tradition in my young life. As a kid growing up, change was my constant companion. Another rent house in the wrong part of town, or a cropper's shack, to be approached with misgivings, on someone else's farm; new teachers who considered me extra after-school work for them, and kids who never chose me for their teams. Yes, the annual Milton family reunion was the carrot I hopped to every year until that one time.

That night and for years afterwards, I couldn't name it, but it brought something unfamiliar and repellent to my young life. Something that grew into trepidation, even for my father, and especially for my prospect of sex that didn't serve me well until years later.

I can smell it still. The attic where all the kids slept together. Aunt Jean didn't use it except for storage and yearly family reunions, so the air was old and the thread-bare sheets on all the beds were musty, but none of us kids cared one bit. I loved seeing again the homemade quilts made from scraps my aunt confiscated from family and friends, and not even the stale smell of them dampened my happiness.

This was my only sense of home. I could depend on everything about the weekend being the same every year. I looked forward to seeing my mother smile. It is the only memory I have of her smiling. The entire family would all be sitting around the bonfire before bedtime. She always had a baby in her lap, and sometime she would even laugh out loud. That was so great. If I ever loved her at all, it was then.

That night Mother had my skinny body washed clean of the day's animal smells, but instead of waiting for my sister, I dashed ahead of her up the dark, steep stairs. I was the first kid to hit the attic and I took pride in that. I scanned the beds to decide which one would be mine. I didn't see that I wasn't alone, but I got wind of barn, horse, and body odor at the same time he pulled me down onto the nearest bed. An unfamiliar voice whispered to me, and my first thought was, "How strange. Uncle Ken doesn't whisper."

My childhood trust and love was still intact until I turned my head to look at his sun-aged face. The one dim lamp on the old corner table didn't shed much light. I sensed, rather than saw, a stranger. His rough cowboy hands were now on my body in a new way. His familiar eyes were blank. Hot, fast breath on my face paralyzed me. Within seconds he found his prey. He jerked my cotton gown up almost over my head. His rough hand was rubbing me up and down while he held me still with his knee. Something smooth and hard was going in me. I didn't—couldn't—make a sound, but it sure did hurt. It was my sister bouncing into the room that stopped him.

But I wasn't saved.

The next morning when I came downstairs, he wasn't still eating breakfast, thank goodness, but as I walked to the barn with my cousins, his cheerful howdy stopped me cold. I didn't know what to do with my mind. I couldn't believe it, but Uncle Ken was his usual self. There was no proof that last night's seconds had ever happened. He offered to help me up into the saddle as he always did, but without a word, I turned back to the house in confusion. Something I couldn't grasp had changed my idea of myself. Something that would take me a long time to understand.

As the days grew into weeks and then months, my confusion changed into dread. Never would I be alone with Dad, if I could help it. I would scream as loud as I could whenever my older brother even touched me. I wouldn't give my male teachers eye contact. I didn't believe one word any minister said. And Mother had herself a helper with the baby at every family reunion after that.

If Uncle Ken or Dad or Mother or any other adult noticed the change in my behavior, no one ever said anything. And I certainly didn't let on.

Years later, when Mother gave me the "Now Edna Arretha, just remember, they won't buy the cow if they can get the milk free" sex education lesson, I understood for the first time that being a woman, I had something a man had to have. It didn't even have much to do with him or the female on the receiving end of it.

It was beyond his control. No sir, it didn't have much of nothing to do with who you were or where he was or who he was. Nope, sex was a trivial matter. Nothing to give undue deliberation.

———

It didn't take no time to pack me and my few duds on a bus to California. I was so excited I didn't sleep a wink the whole trip. It all happened so fast. I was gettin' out of that Oklahoma shack to live with my brother's family in sunny California. Lord, I was all aquiver. That first morning at my brother's house, the breakfast smells woke me up off their living room couch. I didn't wait to be called. I got right up to find the bathroom to pee and wash my face. I smiled at my happy face in the mirror because I felt sure as shootin' that at last, my life was gonna be kicks. That was five days ago.

"But I'm just barely sixteen. I ain't old enough to get married. And I'm thinkin' it's likely against California law," I whined.

"Well, you got that last part right," my brother said through his grin. "But that ain't gonna be no problem. All I have to do is write our ma a letter for her permission and you are a married woman."

"Why didn't you tell me, before I came all the way out here to live with you, the first thing you'd do is marry me off? In your letter, you told Ma I'd be goin' to school and helpin' out with your kids. Not one damn word about gettin' married."

I had never much liked this older brother, so

the only reason for leavin' Oklahoma's dust at his invitation was because California looked so pretty. I loved the pictures of it in books. My dream was to get the schoolin' I needed for a right good job. I could buy pretty new clothes, wear lipstick and nail polish. I'd make a mighty fine California girl.

But now, only a week later, I watched my brother shovel in the pork chops, potatoes, and gravy his tired wife had waitin' for him the minute he stepped into the kitchen. Betrayal and wariness filled my heart. How could this man be in charge of me so completely? Did him being a man make it right? It was sure lookin' like I didn't have no say. And it had all been so fine when I first got here.

Brother Earl's house was in the area called Tortilla Flats, an excitin' place. Nothing like the small towns or dirt farms of Oklahoma. I saw all kinds of folks livin' along Figueroa and Garden Street: working class Mexicans, Chumash, niggers, and dustbowl whites. And of all things, famous bands like Tommy Dorsey and Chuck Berry even came to town to play. People smiled at me when I walked down the street, and folks sittin' on their front porches were friendly.

It could work out. Sure, the house was too small for five people. Anyone could see that. But it was a fair sight better than anything I had ever lived in.

My favorite room was the living room. Big blue flowered wallpaper and maroon-and-white striped linoleum on the floor. A kitchen that would do and, of all things, the bathroom was in the house. The couch made a fine bed, and there was no sharing it with anybody.

All these new wonderful things prompted me to beg, "I can get an after-school job and weekends, too. I'd give most all my salary to ya. Wouldn't that be a help? And I don't eat much. I'll be no trouble at all. Please, for God's sake, don't turn me over to some man."

"Edna, that's enough. My lord, you'd think I was selling you off into slavery, the way you're carrying on. You haven't even met my friend, so quit with your walleyed fit. I'm thinking the two of you will get on just fine."

His chair made a complaining noise as he stood up and wiped his mouth on his sleeve. A slow nod at his wife with a, "I'll be home directly," and he was out the same screen door he had come in, just a little while ago.

The woman turned to the sink and bent over the dirty dishes as she quietly cautioned, "Just give it up, Edna Arretha. Ain't no woman I know have any say in how things go. Don't 'spec you'll be the first."

His name was Charles, but everyone called him Red. He didn't have a Chinaman's chance with me, even if he hadn't been freckle-faced, short, and skinny. However, he didn't seem to notice, instead he just went on and on about his good-paying job and the apartment there in Ventura that "needed a woman's touch."

Hell, I thought, as I stared at his moving mouth. Can't he see I ain't no woman?

Red loved having a captive audience, so his words just flowed forth. I don't think he even noticed or cared I only caught one, now and then. And I never had nothin' to say back. He done all the talkin'.

"Damn, Edna. I got me a mighty fine job with tha Shell Oil Co. You know what a roustabout does? Course you don't, gal. Well, I'm tellin' you, I stay mighty busy. With cleaning tools, and moving supplies to the worksite and then with all the servicing I do, I never stop. My favorite job is mixin' the drilling mud. You're going to find out how dirty my clothes get. And where I work has the reputation for trouble, but it is the 12th most productive field in the whole damn country. It covers over three thousand acres of steep hills. The roads I have to travel to well pads and tanks make lots of switchbacks. It's dangerous livin', just getting from one place to another. But what makes it nice is the Ventura River runs from Ojai and cuts through it to the Pacific Ocean. The riverbanks is covered with chaparral and coastal sage scrub and woodland, and those hills hide it from Ventura. There is a company camp house where Shell throws parties for all us employees. Lots of beer drinkin' and dancin' going on just about once a month. Yep, and with sixty cents an hour, I'm 'bout in clover."

His hand reached for mine as he declared, "All I'm needin' is a wife to take care of me and the kids that will be comin' along. Now, don't play hard-to-get. As soon as your ma sends that permission letter back here, we'll get hitched. Don't stare at me like that, gal. Can't you tell when you is well off?"

The letter came and that was the finish of it. Certainly there was no church wedding, and afterwards, not more than a few neighbors gathering for beer and loud music in the bare, small back yard. Somehow it was like I wasn't there. I didn't pay no mind to which dress I got out of my suitcase to wear. Then, when I stood in front of the judge who married us, I didn't hear a word he said.

Back at my brother's house, everyone laughed and teased me, insistin' I drink some beer, but I couldn't swallow. I couldn't talk neither, not that anyone cared. Only my sister-in-law really looked at me, and her eyes were full of unspoken dread.

I couldn't feel myself at all. Honest to God, it was like I wasn't there. When I stood in the shower at Red's apartment with the cool water runnin' over my head, the storm came. The water forced me into my new life.

My mouth opened and the loud bawlin' that poured out startled me. What had happened? Where had I been? Where was I now? Married! Oh God Almighty, I'm married. Married as hell.

That was all I could recollect. Right away, my wailin' turned into whimpers when Red's fists started beatin' on the bathroom door. "Cut out that damn racket and get your skinny ass out here. I got something to show you," he yelled. "I mean it, gal. You won't like it if I have to come in there after you."

I wonder if Red was proud of what he had to show me. I sure couldn't see nothin' worth the mention of it. There he stood all red-faced and naked, with his talley-wacker pokin' out through the thin pale hair all around it.

I might have laughed if I wasn't so ailin' because it looked just like a Vienna sausage. There was nothin' to do but go to the bed. I was woman enough to know I best not rile him.

I saw his eyes just long enough to be reminded of

Uncle Ken's. The empty, yet fierce glare of a man at the mercy of his hormones. Without a word, he knocked my knees apart and banged into me with such force that I didn't even think about what I was feelin'. I held my breath and closed my eyes. That helped some.

After his scrawny body got done with that up and down, back and forth rockin' motion he was doin' on top of me, he fell over in a heap. Thank goodness it sure didn't take very long at all. Probably not more than a minute, but that was too long. I laid there still as death.

Was he done? Was he gonna say something now? Silence.

Within a few minutes I could tell by his breathin' that he was asleep. I dared to slide off the bed and into my cotton gown. Enough light came from the street to guide me into the living room. I melted down into the only chair. It was by the window. The moon was out and the street was empty.

I leaned into the window screen. It took a while before I come to myself. I'm sixteen, was my only thought. Only sixteen.

When I didn't get pregnant, month after month, I finally got Red to agree to let me go to work. With a greasy spoon over a few blocks, I could walk to work, and takin' hamburger orders for forty cents an hour sounded better than what I did with my days now.

Since Red never gave me no money, except for groceries, all I could do was walk around Ventura for entertainment. That's how I spotted that most beautiful building. If only they hired girls for ushers, then I could have had me a real good job.

The Mayfair Theatre on the corner of Ash and Santa Clara was the finest place in all of Ventura. I would stand outside and admire its gold crown with the white space in the middle for the marquee. I'd stare at the pictures of all the stars, and the little girl in me would pretend to work there. I would make the best usher ever. There would be popcorn to eat and I'd get to see the movies.

Red never had enough money for me to go any place with him. Besides, I'd be in the way of his beer drinkin' down at the Sportsman on California Street after the show.

I learned not to walk downtown past Rain's Shoes and Edie's Treasure Room because it only made me feel gloomy to see all the windows full of beautiful things I couldn't buy. Instead, I walked on up to the Mission San Buenaventura. It was very beautiful and peaceful and I loved it there until I learned what the name meant. City of Good Fortune built in 1782.

I'd sit there on the bench and stare at the statue of Father Junipero Serra and think about how I could have had good fortune in Ventura. I could be studyin' in high school and swimmin' at the beach and laughin' with girl friends. But no, instead my life was shit, and all because my sorry ass brother married me off.

Waitin' on hungry men wasn't any fun, but at least I didn't mind so much until Red decided he needed my whole weekly check. What was the point, I'd ask myself, as I walked home to make his dinner. I lived for those days of the month when he worked graveyards. That way I didn't have to sleep with him or listen to him eat.

He wasn't too pleased with my progress as a wife, either. "Can't you do something besides just lay there like a sack of potatoes? The only good thing about your ass is that it ain't costing me nothing."

I thought about sayin', "And now my line is, 'Oh, my darling. Please give it to me again'?" I was mad as hell, and I knew Red didn't hesitate to beat me any time he felt like I deserved it. Best to keep my mouth shut and that is what I usually did.

He never stayed in the apartment long anyway. He ate and slept and poked me almost every day. That was about it. I made his meals, but never sat down with him. At first he forced me to, but finally it got to where he didn't notice.

And sex? Sex was a wordless few seconds of him emptyin' himself into me.

I can't say what got into me. I mostly never said nothin' to him, but this time his usual 'get your skinny ass in bed' just ripped me good. I didn't move one inch.

Red looked surprised at the hate and disgust I knew he saw in my eyes. All the misery built up in me over the past four months just screamed out, all on its own. I stood right there in the kitchen and yelled, "You sorry son-of-a-bitch. How about instead of me takin' my skinny ass to bed, you take your skinny ass out of here and poke your sorry little thing into someone else?"

He moved too fast for me. Before I could run, he had me by the hair and I regretted my words. Instead of just slappin' me around, like he usually done, he let go of my hair, took his fist, and hit me in the stomach.

For sure, I was in trouble. That's about all I recollect. I do remember bendin' over from the pain in my middle and then the next thing I know, I'm flyin' through the air. My face hit the corner of the stove, so I'm told, but I didn't feel nothin'. All I know is that the hospital was a wonderful place to wake up in.

"How are you feeling this morning?" The doctor smiled.

When I didn't answer, the doctor spoke again. "Your husband brought you in yesterday evening. He said you had taken a fall and he couldn't wake you up."

"Where is Red?" was all I could manage.

"I don't know, but he isn't here. Can you tell me what happened to you?"

"Not unless you can tell me that he isn't comin' back to get me."

The doctor pulled up a chair to the side of the bed and looked closely at me. "Edna Arretha, you have suffered a concussion and you have been raped. So no. Your husband won't be coming to get you."

Raped. So that's what Red does to me.

The very next mornin' this police lady came to see me. I didn't know I could be such a talker. There hadn't ever been no one in my life to talk to. The customers just gave me their orders without any chitchat; even when I saw my brother or sister-in-law, they didn't want to hear anything out of me. And I sure as hell didn't talk to Red. So I guess the friendly lady from the police department got more than an earful.

"I didn't want to marry Red or nobody. I'm only close to seventeen now, but my brother wouldn't let me have no say. So no, lady, I ain't got no family here in Ventura to help me and I ain't got no friends either."

The lady cop smiled. "You are wrong about that last part. I know a lady who may not be your friend, but she is willing to take you in. You will need a place to live while you are getting a divorce, and she has offered to give you a bed for some help with her kid. Her husband is overseas and she needs to work. Her only child is three years old. If you would be willing to take care of this little girl and cook and clean and do laundry, then you can stay at her house."

"Divorce? You said, divorce?"

"Yes, of course. Your husband has agreed to getting it in exchange for you not filing charges against him for battery. That is what you want, isn't it?"

"Oh my God, ma'am. That makes this beatin' well worth it. Yes, yes. Yes to everything. Who is the lady? When do I leave for her house?"

The cop patted my hand. "The lady is the sister of the man who owns the hamburger place where you work. Dorothy lives in an old house not far from the café. It will be another few days before you can leave the hospital, but when you can, she will come get you."

I wasn't alone in that hospital ward, but I had never felt more safe. The darkness made the other bodies invisible, but the night noises of several in unison created a chorus of sound.

I smiled and hugged myself under the covers. I'll be gettin' a new life. No more being married. No more beatings or rapings. With a divorce, I'll now be a grownup. I'll work for room and board until I'm stronger.

Then, by God, I'll find a better job and get on with it. There won't be no man orderin' me around. No tellin' what I can do, given the chance.

For the first time in my life I felt a surge of hope and confidence well up between my young and still growing breasts. I can do this, was my last thought before a sound sleep enfolded me securely.

Dorothy came to see me a couple of days later in the hospital. I wasn't very steady yet, but I did manage to sit up in bed.

"It ain't much of a house, but it's big. Seven rooms, in fact. Belongs to my husband's family. They all dead now. You will have your own room with a lamp and dresser. My daughter, Lilly, mostly sleeps with me, but she too has a bedroom. I 'speck you'll find everything to your liking."

"I'm much obliged to you, Dorothy. You are savin' my life and I can promise you won't be sorry. I'll work right hard for you."

Three days later while drivin' home with Edna and her baby daughter, Dorothy realized she was talkin' too much. "Stop. Glory, I must be nervous. I sound like a commercial," she said to herself, as she took a sideways glance at the stranger in her front seat.

She tol' me later she thought I was sure poorly, but my green eyes were alive. Brown hair, with a hint of red here and there, framed a face that will probably be pretty one day. My being grateful and a hard worker was the important thing.

Her brother had assured her that taking me in wasn't much of a risk, so this was the thing to do. If she don't have to pay a babysitter, and I get all the housework done for her, she'll be better off than she is now.

"Here we are, Edna. Get out and make yourself to home. You'll find your clothes in your bedroom. I got them for you yesterday from Red's." Dorothy moved to get the little girl from the back seat.

Lilly was silent as death. No smiles, but no frowns either. She just looked at her mother with a question mark in her baby eyes.

I closed the car door and turned to survey a vast yard with an old house settled in the middle of it. When I saw the porch swing, I was hooked. Tears came to my eyes and my heart skipped a beat. Sure, the house needed a coat of paint and the flowerbeds were a mix-mash of flower bushes and shrubs that looked like they were set out and then forgotten. But there was a friendly air to the place, and I was happy to be walkin' towards the steps that slanted slightly to the right.

From the living room, I could see into the dining room and the kitchen. They were all the same size, big! The old oval table had six chairs around it, and there was room to dance in the kitchen.

The other side of the house was more confusin', with no hall at all. I had to go from one room to get to the next. My bedroom was off the dining room, and judgin' from the way the floor slanted, it must have been a porch at one time.

Lilly's room was between the bathroom and

Dorothy's. I could easily touch the ceiling in the bathroom, but the bathtub was long and deep and clean.
I loved the white floor and walls. One of the tired pink
towels would be mine.

"I'll make dinner tonight, Edna. Why don't you play
with Lilly on the porch? I want her to get used to you
before I have to leave for work tomorrow."

Lilly took my hand, but the look on her face told me
she wasn't sure about all this. Luckily, two neighbor kids
came runnin' the minute we closed the screen door, so
I didn't have to do anything but make sure she didn't
get hurt. I sat in the swing and didn't take my eyes off
the little girl. For the first time since I laid eyes on her,
she yelled and laughed and ran around like a wild Indian
with her friends.

"Lilly? Where do you want Edna to sit?" Dorothy
said.

"Yonder." Lilly pointed her fat little finger to the
empty chair at the end of the table.

"Thank you, Lilly." I was quick to join in the game.
"What did Mama make us for dinner?"

"Cornbread and potatoes and milk. My favorite."

Dorothy laughed. "You think she's kidding? That
child will never starve as long as there is cornbread."

After I washed the dinner dishes and watched how
Dorothy gave Lilly her bath, I found my way back to
the porch swing. The last of the day was almost gone,
and a very slight breeze swayed the haphazard flowers.
I closed my eyes and offered up a prayer of thanksgiving. I hadn't any notion as to what to say or who might
hear me, but I just couldn't help it. I was so grateful. My

stomach was full, I was safe, and I was alone in the early evening. No horny man to bother me with demands and complaints. I was on my way to being single and my body was getting stronger.

I hadn't thought about it much in my life, but God might be for real. How else could all this be explained?

Lilly turned out to be an easy child to tend. Even without any evidence of an emotional attachment between us, we got on just fine. Our days together, while Dorothy worked, were slow and easy. She ate like a field hand whatever I put in front of her, and the neighborhood kids and playground in the park across the street gave her the exercise she needed.

I never took my eyes off of her, although I noticed one or two of the mothers would sometimes read instead of watchin' their kids. The assortment of other women took no interest in me and that was the way I wanted it.

First of all, I was too young to contribute to conversation about husbands, and obviously I didn't know anything about fashion. After an hour of playin' and then eatin' lunch, Lilly's two-hour nap was a certainty. I used that time to prepare dinner for all of us as well as clean house and do the wash. I didn't want Dorothy to have to do one thing when she got home except enjoy Lilly.

Peaceful is what it was for me. I felt so grateful for the safety and stillness of my life. No customers to wait on at the diner and no damn husband to navigate.

In the evenings after dinner, while Dorothy and Lilly read children's books, I'd sit on the porch swing and smile. The weeks went by with no word from my brother or his wife, and best of all, nothing from Red.

I really didn't exist to anyone other than Dorothy and Lilly. I hated the worry of it, but I knew this new life couldn't last.

What I had sense enough to dread came in the form of a letter from Dorothy's husband. He had been slightly wounded and would be comin' home in another month. She joined me on the porch to tell me about it all.

"I think you know, Edna that I won't need your help after Jim gets back. So you might want to start looking for a job and a place to live pretty soon."

"Yeh, sure. I remember you sayin' I could stay until your husband come home. It's sure been a good thing for me, but I understand I can't stay. I'll see what I can scare up."

Even though I had expected this news, that didn't keep it from hurtin' my heart. These past few months had been the best in my whole life. We weren't family, and that was what I liked. Dorothy treated me with respect, from a distance. Lilly minded me, but never ran to me for a hug.

The absence of emotion was healing. Havin' family wasn't all it's cracked up to be. At least not mine anyway. Not havin' anybody else decidin' for me is the way I'm going to live it, from now on. But now what?

"I need to get out of this swing, Dorothy, if I'm going to figure out what to do. So, since it's still early, I'm walkin' down to the beach for a spell."

"Okay, but don't stay too long. It is safe enough, but you never know. I'll take your place in the swing," she said with a kind smile.

I had all my strength back by now, but it still felt

good to sit down on the beach to watch the waves. The water moved and moved.

Kind of like my life, I'm thinkin'.

Sitting motionless and mindless was all I could do for a time. But eventually, my mind kicked in.

Okay, missy, first things first. A job. Have to have a job before I can rent a room somewhere. And just what in the hell can I do? Wait tables is all I've ever done. Ain't that the shits? No education and won't be gettin' any either.

As the sky turned dark and gloomy, so did my mood. When it was fully dark and time to walk back to Dorothy's, I dusted off my shorts and mumbled to the water, "Well, there is one damn thing for sure. I ain't going backards. I'll not go back to that diner and those same people and hamburgers. If I have to do the same thing, it will be in some new place. Some really special place. Maybe the Sportsman Restaurant and Bar? Why the hell not? I don't look like chopped liver, so I ain't gonna act like it."

These positive thoughts kept me company all the way home.

A few days later on a Sunday afternoon, Dorothy stayed home with Lilly, giving me my first opportunity to walk to South California Street to the Sportsman. I had never been in it, but Red's stories made it sound like a real fancy place. It catered to Shell Oil Company men. To hear him tell it, he was one of their favorite customers.

I wore my best dress, but it wasn't enough to give me the confidence I needed. As I lingered on the side-walk in front of the bar window, I read the sign: Today's specials… Tanqueray Gin Martini and Beefeater.

I had no idea about either, but I stood up taller and opened the door. Inside it was dark and cool, the perfect opposite to the day outside. The long bar was the main attraction. The bar room was narrow, opening up at the end for tables and booths. Serious character with a prohibition feel; it was absolutely beautiful. The ornate mirror behind the bar was breathtakin'. Metal duck lamps adorned some of the booths. Just standing there in that cool, dimlighted bar made me feel all grown up and somehow glamorous. I could feel a smile takin' over my face.

I was totally enchanted with the feel of the place. As soon as my eyes adjusted to the dim light, I walked over to the end of the bar and asked the beautiful bartender if I could speak to the manager.

Right at that very minute the manager came walkin' out of the kitchen and said, "I don't need another waitress right now, but I could use some help in the kitchen. How do you feel about washing dishes and peeling potatoes?"

I didn't like what the manager said, but I liked him. A short, fat man with a big grin.

"Besides," he continued before I could open my mouth, "I'm thinking you ain't old enough to waitress." But his smile was friendly and fatherly.

"I'll be eighteen pretty soon. And, sure mister, I'll work in your kitchen. What you payin'?"

"Forty cents an hour is the going rate. But you can put in long hours if you want to and have enough to get by. When can you start?"

I didn't hesitate before answerin', "Give me a couple of days to find a place to live and to tie up some loose ends." I wasn't even a little happy with this job prospect, so I jumped ahead of myself. "How about as soon as I'm eighteen and there is a need, you let me waitress for you?"

The boss smiled and said slowly, "All right, if you are a good worker, it's a deal."

I could tell what he was thinkin' by the way he looked at me. Why was a pretty young thing like me willin' to work in a kitchen? Shouldn't I be in school and where was my family? He kept his questions to himself, thank goodness, and instead just shook my hand.

"I'll hold you to it," were my partin' words.

But once back into the sunshine I could feel the tears comin'. One thing I prided myself on was not ever cryin' over nothin'. But shit, I'm not even eighteen and completely off the track. How in the world was I going to go from kitchen help to somebody, some day?

As I retraced my steps to Dorothy's, all the hurt and helplessness of my life bore down on me. No education meant no future. I knew that. So why couldn't I get it through my thick skull?

For evidence of my dreams about what I could become, I thought about how I ran Dorothy's house without any problems. I was good at managin' responsibility, so I'm thinkin' I could do the same with something else. But what? And how in the hell am I ever gonna get a chance? I knew for damn sure I wasn't cut out to work in no café for the rest of my life. Waitin' on folks and takin' orders ain't for me. But what is? Questions without answers followed me all the way back to Dorothy's.

Findin' a room to rent wasn't any trouble, but it sure was a let down. No swing; no kitchen; no yard or park to enjoy. Just a tall, old, brown building on the corner of South Oak and East Santa Clara Street.

I could walk to work, but that was its only plus. No sheets or cover on the narrow, sunk-in-the-middle bed in a small room with no chair and only one small dresser that had a you-are-not-a-real-person look about it. The bathroom was down the hall and had to be shared with four other renters. The one window without curtains let in the streetlight and noise.

How long can I stand this? No one cares if I live or die, so why should I? Oh for Pete's sake. It's time I quit this bellyachin' and go to sleep. It ain't like I'm dumb or stupid, so something will turn up. I just got to pay attention.

Right away I decided to eat off the plates before I washed them, but I didn't let anyone see me doin' it. With no other way to make it on my earnings, I never went to bed hungry, and since I didn't have to buy food, I had money for cigarettes. At first lightin' up was only something to do on break, but now they were my only friends. I sat out back of the Sportsman and smoked. Or, I walked to the beach on my one day off to sit and smoke all afternoon.

Probably months went by before I realized that I seldom said a word to anyone or them to me. In the kitchen, all I did was work. I wasn't any more interested in the other workers than they were in me.

At night in my room I just slept. On my day off I went to the beach and wandered up or down for a while, and then sat starin' mindlessly at the water. Not much of a life, but it was doable. As long as there was no man barkin' orders and pokin' his thing at me, I could make it.

Workin' in the kitchen, I never saw Red or my brother, if they came in. But change came, thanks to takin' my cigarette break somewhere other than in the restaurant alley.

The sidewalk bench, just a little ways down the street next to the bus stop, was my new place to smoke. And that day I would have turned around and headed to the alley if he hadn't jumped to his feet when I walked towards the bench.

"It's okay, miss. I'm just here for another minute or two. The bus should be along directly."

I had to drop my eyes. If I kept lookin' at him, I was sure he would know my thoughts.

God Almighty! Never had I seen such a man. Tall, suntanned, trim, friendly gray eyes, and probably about my age.

I paused, but didn't move any closer, so he said in a quickened voice, "I'm a student pilot stationed at the Oxnard Air Force Base. I come into Ventura on my days off to have a beer and maybe a visit with someone. I'm missing my folks and hometown something awful. You from around here?"

"I'm from Oklahoma, but I been hereabouts for almost two years now." The words just came out of my mouth on their own. My feet took over then and moved me to the bench. "I'm on my cigarette break. I usually sit here for a spell."

He sat down after I did but said no more. It was like we were soakin' each other up and words would have gotten in the way. Seconds passed as I lit my cigarette, blew out the smoke, and then was grateful I thought of something to say. "Where is the air force base?"

He smiled at me and quickly said, "It's in Camarillo, California. I'd say about fifteen miles out of Ventura. You live in Ventura?"

"I do. My name is Edna Arretha Milton. What's yours?"

Was I being forward? I had no idea. Never had I been in such a fix. Could he see my chest heavin' up and down? My hands were shakin', too, and my voice sounded scratchy and strange. Oh God, help me know what to do, I prayed until I realized he was answerin' me.

"I'm Ben Groves from Creede, Colorado, and I'm powerful glad to make your acquaintance. You work around here, do ya?"

Thank God, the bus was comin'. All I had time to say was, "Yeah."

"I'll be back on Sunday. Edna Arretha Milton, will you meet me here at this bench around ten o'clock?" As he leaned above me, the best smile I have ever seen took over his face.

My strange voice said, "If I can get off, I will." Absolutely nothing else would come out of my mouth.

I watched him climb onto the bus. He turned and waved at me before it rolled away. I threw down my cigarette and then mindlessly lit another one.

"Oh God, oh God! What just happened?" I gasped.

I couldn't sit another minute. Standin' wasn't enough

either. I must have been a sight spinnin' around and around and huggin' my skinny self.

As soon as I got back to the kitchen, I found my boss. He just rolled his eyes in disbelief and then broke out with a 'I know what's up' look when I asked off from 10 am to 2 o'clock. What did I expect? The man had never seen me smile before. He smiled at me and agreed that I could make up the time after closin'. Then would be a good time to give the kitchen, and especially the stove, a deep cleaning.

That night in bed when I closed my eyes, Ben's face appeared. That smile. Those eyes. How could I make myself more presentable? All I could think of was to wash my hair and take a fresh shirt to put on. I sure wasn't gonna smell like a kitchen if I could help it.

The time before Sunday was new, too. Had the grass always been this green? What was I doing smilin' at the Mexican bus boy? Might I find a shirt at the Salvation Army resale store to go with these old shorts? Happiness. Is this what happiness feels like?

Come Sunday I was sittin' on the bus bench waitin'. Ben's sparkling eyes danced as he stepped off the bus and moved toward me. "I've been bustin' to see you again, Edna Arretha Milton".

Encouraged to think I could speak and give an acceptable reply, I said, "I'm pleased to see you again, too, Ben Groves. It is Groves, isn't it?"

"Yep, Groves from Creede, Colorado, where I'm going back to as soon as they turn me loose."

"I want to hear all about it. Where can we visit? I have to be back to work at two." Silently I prayed, don't ask me where I work.

Ben looked me in the eyes and said, "I thought we'd just walk down to the beach. Get a lunch near to the pier. What'd you think?"

"Good. That would be good."

But then the walkin' was awkward. I was either a step ahead or a step behind. I didn't know what to do with my hands. A cigarette would be good, but I didn't like to walk down a street smokin'.

"May I have your hand? We're coming to a cross street and I sure can't have nothing getting you."

I didn't have a thought. Decidin' was beyond me. I paused to look Ben directly in his eyes.

He wasn't smilin'. He reached for my hand and I gave it. "Now you're safe."

My new life began at that moment.

"I've never heard no nothing about a Creede, Colorado. You got to tell me what it's like."

We sat at a table on a wide covered porch at the only café close to the pier. I could feel the warm steady breeze movin' my long brown hair. The only thing I could do was look out to the water. Maybe he'll say something in a minute.

From Ben's side of the table, it seemed his thoughts ran a mile a minute. He couldn't take his eyes off me. Who was this beauty, they wanted to know. My cold green eyes now must'a been shimmerin' with life. A mouth that didn't quite know what to do with a smile. A tall, trim body that said hold me and don't dare, all at the same time.

He later admitted to thinking, talk about Creede, you

fool, until you can get yourself under control.

"Well, Edna, I'll tell ya. It's a mighty fine place and it's where I'll spend the rest of my life once this war is over. California is pretty, but you have never seen the likes of the mountains and rivers we have in Colorado. The hunting and fishing is the best. Long hard winters are tolerable because the summers are so beautiful. Silver was discovered back in 1869. In fact, it was re-named for the man who discovered the Holy Moses Mine there. You want to hear the story?"

"Sure do."

My God, he asked me if I want to hear his story. Red never did as much. I may just bust from happiness, right now this minute.

"Okay. First was the Holy Moses, then the Amethyst, the Bachelor, and later the King Solomon. These heavy-producing rich mines made Nick Creede a millionaire. But his health gave out at a fairly early age and he was forced to sell his properties and move to a lower alti-tude. He finally settled here in California. He took his own life at the age of fifty-six. It is said he killed himself because of his wife. He divorced her, but she insisted on living with him anyway."

"Divorce, you say?" My voice is giving me away, I'm sure of it.

"That's the story. I don't know nothing about divorce. My folks fuss and fight, and then they laugh and hug each other up. Not being married myself, I can't really judge, but I'm thinking it all boils down to the loving. The whole thang is the loving. And it is either there or it ain't. I never been in love yet, but I plan on it. How about you?"

I looked toward the sea, away from his questioning eyes. Secrets. I guess there will have to be secrets.

I could feel his eyes on me, so I turned back. "Lovin' someone special would be the best life, I'm sure of it. Please excuse me a minute. I'll be right back."

I got out of my chair too fast and then I stumbled around lookin' for the ladies room sign. I could feel his eyes follow me as I shoved open the bathroom door. After splashin' cool water on my face, I looked at myself in the mirror.

So it doesn't show? No one in this world loves me, and it doesn't show?

Ben stood up to pull back the chair for me when I returned to our table. How will life ever be any better than this? Food served to me and paid for by another; waves rollin' in onto white sand under the May mid-day sun, and a man smilin' at me like no other.

As I pulled my chair forward, I decided to bury my bruised heart and jump into conversation. "So, the air force is teachin' you how to fly a plane? How is it you want to do that? Sounds mighty scary to me." A big swig of iced tea and a cigarette helped.

Ben smiled and finished his first beer. "I can tell you exactly how it happened. I was still in school, probably the seventh grade. In a one-room schoolhouse, and we were all sitting quiet like and studying when I heard a noise totally strange. It kept getting a little louder and finally, the teacher said, 'Oh, an airplane.'

"Then she let us all go outside into the winter day to watch it. That was the first airplane any of us had ever seen. The next day we learned the plane was flying medicine to Silverton where there was an epidemic of diphtheria. Silverton was isolated from the rest of the country that winter by some big snow slides on the railroad tracks and roadways."

After our lunch we found a shaded place under the pier to watch the waves. The silence wasn't an awkward unwanted one. We both needed the same thing. Enough time to feel the magic between us.

We sat close, but not touchin', and Ben made no move to do so. I stared at the water with my chin on my folded arms that rested on my bended knees, and didn't smoke. Ben didn't either. We were in each other's heads. Somehow without any effort on my part, I had gone from nervous anxiety to the calm that certainty brings. I needed to get back to work at the Sportsman, but that thought wasn't a bother. No more worries about how to get ahead, or how to manage life on my own. Without Ben sayin' a word, I knew he too was feelin' the same as me. We had found each other. It's gonna be down hill from here on out.

I was about five minutes late walkin' in the back door, but no one said a word to me. I threw on my apron and got right to work. The pile of dirty dishes was waitin'. Not even the awful filthy stove could dampen my spirits. Baked-on grease was everywhere, but it didn't matter. I wasn't sure my feet even touched the floor. I felt light as a feather and my heart was swollen with more joy than ever before in my seventeen years.

Hours later, I was alone in the closed Sportsman, workin' like the hired hand I was, yet lovin' every breath

I took. We had found each other. This was it, and we both knew it. Nothing had been said… no need. I would live out my life with Ben Groves in Creede, Colorado.

As I locked the back door, I looked out into the night with new eyes. My pitiful life would be over when the war was. He would come back for me and take me with him to Colorado. He would be my family until I died an old woman. His family would love me, like mine hadn't.

"Thank you, God," I said as I looked up to the heavens. "You must be real for this to have happened to me. I'm gonna make you proud. You'll see."

My life now revolved around Ben. Long close hugs and sweet, soft goodbye kisses was as far as he went. That got my attention. Too, his stories were wonderful. He had so many and because I kept him busy tellin' about his world, there wasn't time for mine. That was my plan.

"I have always wanted to go to school, but you say you didn't?" I said.

"Lord, no." And Ben was off into another story. I could listen forever to his rich, deep voice and his sideways smile that gave life to his rural roots.

"There just ain't no way to describe the discomfort of a pair of new, tight boots on feet that have been exposed to Mother Nature since the snow melted in the spring. New boots and being confined inside a closed classroom was pure torture." Ben frowned and shook his head.

"One day I was well on my way to school, almost had town in sight, and I fully intended to complete the trip when to my good fortune, I heard the tinkling of bells and the clanking of tent poles bumping the ground.

Sure enough, it was a band of sheep on the way to the San Luis Valley for winter range. It didn't take a minute for me to decide to step in behind the whole bunch to help drive the sheep. Just west of the cemetery, I had my school lunch while the herders ate theirs. In the afternoon the herd crossed the river at Wason Ranch and camp was made there. This was a good location because the sheep had water and the stock pens were close for loading them on the morning train. I stayed for supper with the herders. We ate fried mutton cubes, buñelos and hominy, and hot coffee. Now, that's a meal that will stick to your ribs.

"After supper I had to hightail it home. The cows needed milking. I had walked just a little ways when the section crew came up the track heading for Creede. They gave me a ride on the handcar to town. All together it was a very satisfying day. Nothing like school would have been.

"My ditching school went on 'til election day. My folks always went to town on that day and it was just my luck they ran into my teacher. Man alive! Did I get a licking. I'd missed about seven weeks of school. After that, either Mom or Dad walked me to school every damn day." He ended with a laugh.

It was hard to tell which of us was having the most fun. Me listenin' or him tellin'.

Ben got into town to see me every four days. For the first few weeks, it went okay, but I couldn't keep takin' off work, so that was the excuse we needed for him to start meetin' me at my place, after work.

The first time he saw the awful room where I lived,

I had to come clean. Not completely, but I had to tell him some part of my story.

"Ben, let's go sit on the front steps. It's time I told you about me."

We sat down outside because there was no chair for him to sit on in my room and I lit a cigarette. I took a deep breath and began. "I'm seventeen and you're the first good thing that has ever happened to me. My life ain't much and never has been. My family don't live in no wonderful place like yours. They are in dirt-poor Oklahoma. I came to California last year to live with my brother, but that didn't work out. So, to keep a roof over my head, I work in the kitchen at the Sportsman. I ain't got no schoolin' and no good prospects."

I paused my story and gazed into Ben's solemn face. The sun had just gone down and a cool breeze kept us comfortable. I ended my confession with the only truth I was willin' to share. "I'm what they call white trash in Oklahoma."

Ben grabbed my hand. "You ain't in Oklahoma! And you ain't here in California for long neither. I'm taking you home with me. You hear? As soon as this war is over, I'll be back for you. Then you won't ever be alone again. You'll have me to your dying day."

Then his smile came back and he said in a playful tone, "You coming peaceable?"

A dam of tears came without any warning. I cried and laughed all at the same time. With Ben's arms around me, I knew I'd never be afraid again. Only when another renter said, 'excuse me', did I realize what a scene we were makin'.

"Ben, come on upstairs with me. You are stayin' the night." I opened the door and felt small standin' just inside the room beside Ben.

"There is enough light, don't you think?" he said. "That one bare light bulb hanging down from the ceiling makes the room even uglier than it is."

"No light needed." I could feel his smile rather than see it. "My bed is narrow and it sinks in the middle."

Why am I talkin', I wondered.

"Let's stand here a minute, he said. "I want to look at you."

My blouse and shorts dropped to the floor. His clothes joined mine. I stood stock still as his hands gently moved from my face to my neck, then to my breasts, and then on down both sides of my body, as far as his arms could reach.

The window light was just bright enough for me to see his soft and lovin' eyes. He pulled me close and lingered there with his face buried in my hair. A slight something ran down the inside of my leg.

"You are a prize," Ben whispered, as he swept me up in his arms and into the bed.

From then on, our time together revolved around seein' movies, eatin' at the pier café, and makin' love. I was alive and my body no longer felt heavy.

At last I got to go in the Mayfair Theatre, not just stand outside and admire it like I had to when I was married to Red. The movie, *Anchors Aweigh*, with Frank Sinatra, Kathryn Grayson, and Gene Kelly was such a thrill to watch. And too, I liked *The Bells of Saint Mary* with Bing Crosby and Ingrid Bergman.

"What are your thoughts about God?" I said as we walked to my room after the movie.

"Well, let's see. I guess the truth is I don't think about Him at all. He has just always been there, kind of like Ma and Pa. God's a comfort, is all."

"I guess," I sighed. "Glad it don't take no thinkin' about. Never been told nothing except that I'd better watch myself."

"Oh yeah, there are those who like to scare you up with all the 'going to hell' talk. I don't give it no mind. Don't allow I could figure it out no way, so why try."

Ben grabbed me and swung me around and around as if I weighed no more than a pillow. "Now, I can tell you what I do think about. Just all the time. Almost every damn minute. Probably gonna get myself killed for not paying attention."

"And I'm sure I don't know what that could be." I adored the way he always got around to how we made love. "Just so you know, if you're trying to wear me out, you ain't makin' no headway. Now put me down so I can race you home."

There was no way to know how much time we had. So we didn't talk about it. The only thing between us and our life together in Colorado was the damn war. And what could we do about that?

It was June now and gettin' wet at the beach was the only way we stayed cool. By now, the other renters just stepped around us on the porch. No way we could stay in that room with the heat. But after the love makin', we would walk to the beach to cool off and sleep on the damp sand. With me in Ben's arms, I was safe.

I'd never had to do much askin' to get a story out of Ben, but tonight he was not in a talkin' mood. We lay on our backs on the beach, all wet and cool and waitin' for sleep.

Finally he started in. "You asked me the other day if there are any women in Creede who run a business? Women who are independent and without a man?"

"Don't make it a bother. Was just wonderin', that's all."

"Well, sure there was. I recollect Kristina Mattsen ran the Holy Moses boarding house while jest a young girl new in the United States and jest out of Sweden. She could neither speak or understand much English, but she managed very well. Later on she married a Mr. Marten. I've heard she had the first washboard in Creede, brought in on a load of merchandise from Crestone, Colorado, by Mr. Major. The miners and crew at the Holy Moses respected and admired Kristina very much."

I was so glad he was doin' his usual talkin'. I kind of felt that something was wrong, but I didn't want to say nothin' so I just waited him out.

"During the time of the most exciting boom and greatest activity, prospectors were scattered all over the rural area around Creede. So several ladies moved to the mines and boarded miners. They sure worked hard for their money, but it was their business, and done their way. That's what a business is, a service some need.

"And, of course, there were the Fancy Girls. I heard it said several times when I was small that they lived in Creede, but they would rent a saddle horse from the livery stable and pay a call on the rural boys. Quite often today you will see or hear of some business advertising pick up and delivery. Well, this was just delivery."

Ben's laugh helped me relax. Maybe I was just imaginin' things. Maybe nothing was the matter. But Ben didn't go to sleep. And if I did, it wasn't much or for long. I finally sat up to watch the sun come up out of the water.

"Edna, they're moving me out. I'll be gone to the Pacific war by this time next week."

I didn't know I cried out, but why else would Ben be hushin' me? He pulled me up tight to his body and rocked me ever so gentle. We stood up, locked in each other's arms, without a breath between us. The pain of it all finally forced us down onto the sand again. Between kisses, I could hear Ben's insistent voice repeatin' a command.

"Edna, my darling girl, you wait for me right here in Ventura. I'll be coming for you. Nothing but death will keep that from happening. Edna, say it! Say 'I'll be coming for you'."

I mumbled into his chest, "You are coming for me. You will be back."

"Okay now, jest you remember. If I don't come back, then you know I'm dead. For certain, Edna, I'll be dead."

Ben saying the 'dead' word was too much. There was no controllin' my thoughts. I cannot live without him. God better know that.

In a flash I went from being paralyzed with fear and dread to temper. My breath and thoughts were comin' quicker. Ben has to come back for me. The only way my life is gonna count for anything is if I'm married and having his babies.

I raised my head up to look him straight in the eyes. "I'll be awaitin'. You jest get yourself back here to me. We got a lotta livin' to do back in Colorado. You are my life, Ben Groves, and that's all there is to it."

I Do This
Real Good.
Over and Over.

Ben was gone. No more nights sleepin' on the beach in his strong arms; no more twisted sheets and hot bodies in my narrow bed; no more Colorado stories. Just day followin' day in the kitchen at the Sportsman. The radio was now my life.

Since the war in Europe had ended on May 8, all the news was about where Ben was, the Pacific. It sounded so awful. On June 22, the US troops finally captured Okinawa after 82 days of bloody battle. American forces suffered more than 12,000 dead or missing, and more than 36,000 wounded. The Japanese didn't believe in surrenderin'. Accordin' to the talk at the Sportsman, this island hoppin' was a slow go. And the price tag in American lives was too high.

On July 26, the Allies issued the Potsdam Declaration. We could hear the news on the kitchen radio above the cookin' noise. This declaration called on Japan to surrender its armed forces unconditionally or risk 'prompt and utter destruction'.

"Oh God, God, this is good, isn't it? They'll surrender now, won't they"? I directed my question to José, the Mexican busboy.

Of course he didn't speak much English, but he was the only one in the kitchen who ever smiled at me. "Sí, sí, Miss Edna. It's bueno, good."

José and I were partners in crime. I ate from the plates before I washed them, and he packaged uneaten food to take home. He was just a kid, maybe fifteen. Sometimes he would take his break when I did. José didn't talk, but it was nice to have someone sit and smile at me. Especially now that Ben was gone and neither cigarettes nor food tasted the same.

My dishwashin' wasn't going so well either. I had never been sickly, but these days the smells in the kitchen made me throw up. It was down right embarrassing. In fact, I missed the first announcement of the B-29 Enola Gay droppin' the world's first atomic bomb on Hiroshima. It was August 6, and I was in a dead faint on the kitchen floor.

"Edna, gal. Are you in trouble?"

It took me a minute to recognize my boss's voice. But I knew instantly what he meant. "Yes sir, I am. But it ain't trouble. Ben will be comin' back for me as soon as he can. We will get married and then I'll be leavin' here for Colorado."

Sayin' it out loud and to someone made me better right away. I was thrilled to be carryin' Ben's baby. We would be a family from the very beginning. As soon as this damn war was over and Ben got back to me. Till then, I mustn't lose my job.

"You ain't gonna fire me, are you? I'll get past this bein' sick and I won't miss one day of work. Besides, no one can see me here in the kitchen. I've got to keep this job. Ain't no one here in Ventura who cares if I live or die."

"Okay, okay. Don't get yourself all worked up. Sure you can stay. You are a good hand, but try not to faint no more." He patted my cheek like I was a little kid and his smile seemed kinda sad to me. He wasn't gonna fire me, and thank God for that.

Three days later, when the Soviet Union declared war on Japan and invaded Japanese-held Manchuria, I took that as a good sign. The war is going to be over any day now, and Ben will be back. He will be here long before the baby comes in February.

I want us to wait and get married in Creede. Hope he agrees. That is where my life will begin, in Colorado, with Ben and his family and friends. I'll never need anyone or anything else in this world.

I wasn't smokin' no more, and food was beginnin' to taste better. The nights were cooler, too. I looked forward to layin' on my bed and talkin' to Ben just like he was there beside me. I told him about the baby and how I'd be ready the minute he got here.

Then I'd pretend my life in Colorado. Our log house with a front porch swing for our evenings together; a green meadow full of fat cattle that went down to the river; horses in the corral, and tall snow-covered mountains surroundin' us. On Sundays we go to his folks for dinner and Baby Ben would be gettin' hugs and kisses all around. Everyone likes me, too. Ben's kid brother thinks

I'm pretty, and Ben loves me more every day that comes.

When this war is over, when it is over.

I loved my dreams, too. Always Ben was lovin' me. He would smile and gaze into my eyes like he was lookin' for something missin'. His hands were slow and soft on my eager body. And he sounded a 'thank you' sigh when he entered me. Never did he rush at me or hurt me.

Sometimes I cried because he was so wonderful. I hated wakin' up and realizin' the wait wasn't over.

Didn't look like it was a sure thing after all. On August 9 we dropped a second atomic bomb on the city of Nagasaki. Then on August 14, when I heard about the seven hundred B-29s droppin' more than four thousand tons of explosives on military targets in Japan, I just had to cry. For sure Ben was flyin' one.

"Edna, stop it this damn minute," I ordered myself as I walked home from work. "You'll bother the baby if you don't straighten up. Ben ain't gonna die. He can't. Your life depends on it."

I stood up straighter; walked faster, and spoke with authority. "Keep seein' him come in the door. He will be so surprised to see me pregnant, but he will let out a whoop and a holler. We will never be apart ever again. God won't let anything happen to him. He won't."

After a few days, the Japanese emperor got his military to honor his call to surrender, but finally on September 2 a formal surrender ceremony on the USS Missouri in Tokyo Bay ended the war. We passed drinks all around at the Sportsman and everyone hugged everyone. José clapped his hands and smiled all day.

I wasn't a bit tired so I skipped all the way home.

Laughin' and smilin' and greetin' everyone on the street. People came outside, shoutin' at their neighbors and wavin' to me on the sidewalk. I have never been so relieved.

Now Ben would be comin' back to me. Now he would come.

My high lasted for a glorious month or so. It helped to be always reminded by everyone around me and on the radio that it takes time before our troops can get back to the states. Just because the war was over didn't mean Ben would walk in the door.

But why didn't he send me a letter? He could address it to the Sportsman and I'd get it. Why the hell didn't we talk about how he could contact me? We were two stupid kids not thinkin' past the moment.

As the months passed, the questions faded and a lifeless knowin' replaced them. By the time the baby was born, I knew in my heart that Ben wasn't delayed. He was dead.

I didn't start thinkin' about me and the baby real serious like until shortly before labor started. It was supposed to be me and Ben and the baby. I didn't have to know what to do because Ben would take care of me. I would live in Colorado on a ranch with Ben as my world.

So now what? I couldn't wash dishes at the Sportsman as a career. Who would tend the baby? I wouldn't make enough money to hire a sitter. Even if I got to be a waitress, it wouldn't be enough. As my belly grew, my mind stopped plannin' because hope was gone. I seldom thought about anything. Not the baby, me, or Ben. I just drifted through ever passin' day mindless.

It was almost closin' time and I was puttin' up the last of the pots and pans when my water broke. As I stood there holdin' onto the sink, I felt fury for myself take the place of helplessness. Why in hell hadn't I made any plans? Was I gonna think and act like a dependent child when in reality I was a pregnant woman with the responsibility for not only myself but my unborn baby?

I didn't dare call my brother, and I had no money for the hospital. Besides most women have their babies at home. That's the problem, stupid. You have no goddamn home.

I was chokin' on this realization when José bent down beside me. His eyes were anxious and he was speakin' Spanish at a fast clip. I just sat down on the wet floor and buried my head in my hands.

"Edna, Miss Edna, get up." José tugged at my arm. "Pronto. We go to mi casa. José's mama… José's mama."

I looked up into his wide eyes.

He smiled and said, "It's good, good. Mama help."

The amazin' thing is that no one in José's home seemed surprised to see me. Everyone—father, mother, kid sister—were all smiles and assistance.

Relief washed over me and I felt safe and comfortable for a short time. But when labor set in, it was down hill from there.

How can this be? How can anyone live through this kind of pain? Is this what my mother did over and over? I want to die this minute. Please, let me die I begged as the hours drug by. My insides were bein' torn apart, with hardly any time between contractions to breathe or rest.

Mama motioned for me to push. Push! I was crazy with torture. How could I push?

Oh thank God! I'm going to die. I can tell by the way Mama looks at me that something is way wrong. I don't have no strength left, but the pain. God, oh God, stop the pain. After some time passed, I realized I wasn't dead. Shit, I had just fainted.

I could hear a baby cryin', but I couldn't move or think or feel. Blessed unconsciousness rescued me and I don't know how long I was gone. But when I woke up, I was alone in the tiny bedroom. After a minute, I remembered where I was and what had happened. I waited to feel something, but nothing came. The stillness and quiet was wonderful. I wasn't hurtin' either. I felt nothin'. I went back to sleep.

Our baby boy lived only a short time. I was unconscious so I never got to see him or hold him. Best I could make out, José's family buried him. My only contribution was his name, Ben Groves Junior.

As I laid there in someone's bed, the usual family noises resumed. It was Spanish so I have no idea what was said. Mama forced me to eat. José was always there smilin' down at me.

Eventually I graduated to the front porch. I could see there was still a world goin' on around me, but I couldn't speak. Ben was dead. Our son was dead. For all practical purposes, I was an orphan with an orphan's mentality. Since I couldn't talk, I didn't say nothin' to God, but He knew I was thinkin' it. 'You take Ben and the baby and leave me? Ben told me You were a comfort. Guess not.'

"It's time you put me to waitressin'," I said to the Sports-man boss.

He looked shocked at my authority and I was too. Maybe the old me had died along with Ben and the baby. It had been a month now and I had to go back to work.

"Well now, I don't know about that, Edna. You could serve up the hash all right, but I don't think you have the makings of a good waitress."

"What do you mean?" I said between clinched teeth. Was my irritation showin'? "I know how to take food orders and serve customers. I did it for months at the burger place." I knew what he was gettin' at, but I asked anyway.

"You ain't no kid anymore and the men who come in here want more than the food set in front of them. Edna, you just aren't friendly. My customers like to chat it up and make jokes and feel like you are real happy to take their order. That's what I mean."

I sat up straighter on the bar stool, crossed my leg, and let it swing back and forth slowly. Then I leaned forward so that my now larger breasts were shoved to-gether and put a twinkle in my eyes as my mouth formed a flirty smile. "How's this?"

Sure enough, my tired ole boss was impressed with my instant charms. He nodded his head and smiled.

"Look, I need all the money I can make and that means I need good tips. Of course, I'll put on my 'I'm so thrilled you are here' face and play the part. Just give me a chance, will you? I'll take the worst hours and the longest. I ain't got nothing else to do or anybody to do it with."

A couple of weeks after I went to work, Red backed right out the door faster than he came in and my older brother must have gotten the word because he never showed up. Of course, the Sportsman was too rich for his blood, but I was surprised Red gave up his favorite waterin' hole because I worked there.

And it didn't take long for the other Shell guys to stop any talk about me once married to Red. I discovered my talent for controllin' a conversation. It was so easy to redirect anything said and to do it in such a way that no notice was taken. I would smile to myself as I walked away from the table to the kitchen knowin' I wasn't exactly powerless. It felt good to do something with my mind. All those months of washin' dishes and peelin' potatoes were over.

At night when I finally hit the saggin' bed in complete exhaustion, I would marvel at how I was changin'. Clearly the earliest lesson of my life was that I had no one to rely on but myself.

The Sportsman was my whole life. The beach was ruined for me without Ben so I never went there anymore. But at the Sportsman José was my special friend and we shared private smiles as we worked. My boss was thrilled to death with the job I did and the other waitresses were friendly enough.

Especially Sally, the oldest and the Sportsman's favorite. She called all the Shell men by name and never seemed to tire of them or their jokes. And little by little she took me under her wing. Not exactly a mother, but more like a big sister who knew all the answers.

We shared a cigarette break out back of the Sports-man one early evening when Sally first approached the subject. "You do know, don't you, Edna, that you could sure make more than tips."

I looked at her with a half-knowin' smile. "What you talkin' about, Sally?"

"Now don't give me that innocent look. You know damn well what I'm talking about. Men will pay a good price for it."

"Oh, really." The smile left my face. "I don't think I'm cut out for that line of work. Nothing personal, but I've had the worst sex and the best sex there is and I don't see sellin' it as fittin' in between."

Sally just shook her head and said, "God, I know you've had a hard time of it. Everyone knows, but you're wrong. My god, girl, do you ever look in the mirror? You ain't skinny no longer. Since you had the baby, your body has filled out in all the right places and your beautiful brown hair and those emerald green eyes make you a beauty. Don't try to tell me you aren't aware of how men look at you. I've watched you pull them in and then leave them hanging with your remoteness. It's a gift. Being able to signal 'come on' followed by 'not now'."

"Sally, I appreciate you takin' an interest in my life and I'll think about it. But for now, I'm just gonna waitress. Hope you can understand. Ben hasn't been gone long enough. I ain't ready for any man, payin' or not."

How long ago was that conversation? And Sally

hasn't mentioned it since. The newness of waitressin' has worn off and I'm certain sure I don't like it much. The Sportsman is my home and I ain't hurtin' none, but at the same time I'm dead. Dead to any interest in my future or gettin' to know new men.

Ben is still everywhere. When I walk past the sidewalk bench where we met, my heart gets heavier. I can't go to the movies or to the beach either because of my memories of our times together there. I never see my brother or his family, and if it wasn't for José's family, I'd be totally alone outside the doors of the Sportsman.

What damn year is it now, I wonder, as I crawl into my narrow bed. The answer shocks me awake. 1950? I have spent the last four years being a waitress? No home or friends or family?

No life is what I have. No life. I spring out of bed to stand in front of the only window in my rented room.

"Shit! What am I doin'?" I scream to the solitude, not carin' at all if I alarm the renters around me. "Change your life, Edna Arretha Milton. And do it now."

That night instead of dreamin' about Ben, I had a new vision in my sleep. Wheels! Lots of wheels takin' me out of California. Miles and miles of road. Country music on the radio and an ole scruffy driver singin' along.

I woke up with my escape planned and all I needed was for the truck driver I knew to show up at Sportsman. A couple of weeks later, Ole Woody came in. He was his usual jolly self and he headed straight for my station area. I was ready to pitch my idea to him, but first I needed to find out where he was drivin' to next.

"Hey there, Woody, I've been missin' you. Where you back from and where you goin' next?" I poured him a glass of water and handed him the Budweiser he always drank.

"Ah swear, Edna. You get prettier all the time. What you been doing to get that bloom in your cheeks?"

Perfect, I thought, he has sex on his mind. I gave him my loveliest smile and whispered, "Never mind about where you been. What I really want to know is where you goin' and if I can hitch a ride."

I could tell Woody wasn't sure he had heard me right. Never before had I ever talked like this and he had been comin' in here for years. Would he take the bait? God, if only he does.

"I tell you what, you pretty thing. I'll be headed to Galveston, Texas, next week and you sure as hell can keep me company. Now, you serious about this, are you?"

I surprised myself with a gleeful whoop and clappin' hands. "You've got yourself a partner. I'll be right good to you, Woody, 'cause I'm much obliged. Just tell me what day and time and I'll be there. I'll only have one small suitcase since I don't own much of nothin'."

In my room that night, I made myself think about what I was offerin'. Sex. My memories of sex hadn't much faded with time. There was Red with his violent way of coverin' me. Then there was Ben with his tender touch that left me filled up to my heart with love.

This was goin' be different. I'll have to do something with my mind. I'll have to be tellin' myself a story and I won't be able to kiss him. I can't kiss anyone but Ben for now. Maybe never.

José cried when I told him I was leavin'. Everyone else acted like they wished me well. If Sally understood my bargain with Woody, she didn't say so.

As I stepped high to get into the cab, I looked at Woody and was glad to be there. He wasn't bad. Actually I found him to be just a regular guy who tipped really well. His shirt was pulled tight over his growin' belly and his hair was too long for my taste, but I wasn't afraid of him. I'll get to know him some as we ride along. I wonder if that might make it easier?

"Well sir, I've been alone now ever since my wife died back in 1943. We didn't have no children and I don't care much for my family or hers either for that matter. So I just get on down the road and call it a life. What's your story, Little Gal?"

I didn't mind tellin' him. It was a new experience. I hadn't told Red anything because he wasn't interested, and I hadn't told Ben much because I was ashamed of my life. But this Woody guy didn't matter, so I could get it off my chest.

"I was born to poor folks in Oklahoma that I never see no more. I came to California 'cause I thought my older brother in Ventura would take me in, but instead he married me off to a little weasel of a man when I was sixteen. When he raped me all the time, and then beat up on me so bad one time, I ended up in the hospital, the police saw to it I got away from him. I lived in the home of a nice lady and I tended her little daughter while she worked. But her husband got injured in the war and came home, so then I had to find some other place to live and work. That's when I went to work in the kitchen at Sportsman, washin' dishes and peelin' potatoes and such. You sure you want to hear all this?"

"I sure enough do. Beats the hell out of the radio. I get mighty tired of that radio."

"Okay then. I was seventeen when I met Ben. He was trainin' to be a pilot and we only had a few weeks together, but it was the best time of my life. Ben is the only man I'll ever love. I know it positive. But he was killed in the Pacific so he couldn't come back for me like he said. That left me alone to have his baby. It died and I almost did, and since then I've just been workin' at Sportsman these past four years as a waitress. Not much of a life to tell is it?"

Woody looked over at me and shook his head. "No, not much of a life, little lady, not much of a life."

We rode along in silence for over an hour before he had to stop to gas up. When we were on the road again he reached over and patted my leg. "Edna, when I let you out in Galveston, you will know what to do. You are a young thing, but you strike me as someone who can find the best way out. I'd give up waitressing if I was you and come up with something with more of a future."

Woody didn't pay out top dollar for a night's stay in motels, but at least the rooms were clean. After three nights on the road, we rolled into Galveston and by then I was comfortable with the part I played. During the day when we were travelin', I'd spend some time lookin' at magazines with lots of pretty pictures of places and people. Then at night when it was time to go to bed, I'd select one and make up a story with me in it durin' the sex. Woody was clean and he was gentle with me. I didn't even have to tell him not to kiss me. Somehow he knew.

"You okay, Edna?" he'd always say when he was finished.

"Sure, you didn't hurt me none. I'll wash up now and you just get yourself to sleep."

But on the last night he was still awake when I came back to bed. "Do you do it on purpose? Can you be here in the bed with me and yet leave me with the feeling you ain't here at all?"

I laid down slowly before I said, "What do you mean?"

"Your body lets mine into yours, but all the while, you ain't in it. Edna, that gives me a weird feeling and if you don't mind me saying so, if you plan on doing this for a living, you might want to give it a second think."

Do this for a livin'? Is that what I'm goin' do? Be a whore? Have men pay money for me? Get in bed with total strangers day in and day out?

As a tear rolled down my face, I didn't answer. Ben, oh Ben! You died and left me to this?

"What did you say Galveston is called?" I said as Woody's truck rolled down Broadway toward the Texas Gulf.

"Sin City of the South is what I've been told. But some folks call it the Free State of Galveston and that's because gambling, liquor and prostitution are all illegal, but they are tolerated here in Galveston. The houses of prostitution are called 'The Line' and they are from 25th to 30th streets on Post Office Street. It's a lively area due to the sailors who come in on leave and the soldiers from Fort Crockett, not to mention the students at UT Medical Branch and the men who come here regular for business conventions."

Lookin' around at all the oleander bushes along Broadway. I said, "Well, it sure don't look so sinful in the daylight. This Broadway we're on is right nice. Where are you gonna put me out?"

"Right about here. See that statue of a lady pointing her finger? Well hon, you just walk in that direction and you'll find the neighborhood you're looking for. You got a plan, do you? I don't want to have to worry none about you."

"Not really. I'll just walk towards downtown and find me that Post Office Street you mentioned."

I marveled at how calm and sure I sounded even though my stomach was in knots. I waved goodbye to Woody and, carryin' my old suitcase, I walked slowly away, followin' the bronze finger of the statue lady.

'Am I really gonna do this' was the thought that screamed in my head, takin' my attention off the old row houses and palm trees. The sun was Texas hot and plenty humid, but the breeze off the water and the shade from the trees along the sidewalk kept me from bein' too uncomfortable.

As I shifted my suitcase from one hand to the other, I moved towards my next life. A life I had never even considered until the thought of becomin' a fixture in the Sportsman forced my hand. I had my reasons: basically I didn't like to waitress, never had; Ventura was Ben and Ben wasn't comin' back for me; I would never get ahead there because I had no education and no family to fall back on. But being a prostitute is a mighty radical solution. Hell, I don't even know how to spell it, much less how to live it.

I found an old bench outside the Rosenberg Library so I sat for a spell. No hurry. I felt no hurry to get to Post Office Street. What was I gonna do when I got there anyway?

It was the middle of the afternoon and that was about all I knew. What was the month or day or year, for that matter? I felt like I was gone. That Edna Arretha Milton was no more.

As I sat and stared at the still hot day, I had to admit it wasn't the sex part that bothered me. Now, how come is that? But no, sex with anyone other than Ben was just a matter of layin' there and lettin' a man move over and into me. Woody hadn't been no problem at all. I can take myself anywhere I want to in my mind. Even as a little kid I could, and now that I need to, I'll just run off in my imagination until it's done.

Not havin' a long-range plan bothered me the most. Damn if I'm gonna whore all my life. That ain't no plan. Somehow I'll have to learn the business and then I'll buy me a place and manage it. I'll be totally in charge of everything under my roof.

It will be up to me and that is the way it is gonna be from now on. No more waitin' for a man to give me a life. Wars come and go, as do men. In the end, it looks like the only sure way to survive is to escape into the fancy of my mind and put no store on any one man.

I walked to Post Office Street, only to see nothin'

special about it. One hotel or house or store after another on a dusty hot street. Not many people stirrin' either. No palm trees to shade my walkin' up and down with my suitcase. Maybe it would be okay to sit down next to that lady on the street bench.

Might as well give it a try, I thought, as I smiled at her. "Howdy, care if I sit with you here?"

My feet were tired and I was hungry and besides, she was the only person I could see sittin' out in front of a hotel, the Rose Hotel.

"Sure, take a load off, honey. I'm Star and glad to know yah."

In a matter of seconds, I sensed Star must be a prostitute. Her hair was a wild fake blond and her lips too red and her dress had way too many flowers printed on it.

"I'm Edna and I just got into town. Hitched a ride with a trucker from California. Pleased to meet you."

"California? Shit, always wanted to go to California. Why did yah leave?"

"Needed a change of scene I guess. Been there since I was sixteen. Time to move on." I hoped I sounded sure of myself and life.

Star chuckled and then added, "Well, you've landed in one hell of a place. Galveston ain't for the weak or weary. I been here myself since '46. Came after the war. Can't believe it has been five years already. Got to watch the time, it has a way of getting away from yah. You looking for work?"

I gasped at how fast Star talked. And before I could find words she started up talkin' some more.

"Hell, Edna. It don't take much smarts to know you

are looking for work. I been watching you walk up and down this street with that suitcase in your hand. Don't tell me you are one of those gals who is shy about it."

"I ain't shy, just new."

For some reason I liked Star. The woman was no longer pretty, but she wasn't all used up either. Besides it was gonna be dark in a couple of hours.

"Any way you can help me would be appreciated. I don't know one soul here in Galveston and I have no prospects."

Star smiled and offered me a sip of her ice tea. As she watched me gulp down half of it she guessed that the word 'new' didn't come close to coverin' it.

Star didn't hesitate one second to speak her mind. "You are a beauty. Fresh and clean with that 'I'm something' attitude. You'll bring a good price for the first few years anyway. So Miss Edna, this is your lucky day. You are sitting in front of the Rose Hotel where I live and work. I'll introduce you to the madam. She is always on the look out for fresh goods. Pardon my language. Being crass gets to be a habit around here." Star almost looked embarrassed.

Startled, I hesitated then said, "Wait a minute, please, Star. First, could you tell me something about this place? Don't you think I should have some idea of how things work here in Galveston before I talk to the madam?"

"Smart girl. Not just a looker, are you? Okay, see up the street to the east. Notice those fancy houses? That's for the rich menfolks. Folks tell me they are furnished full Victorian and are mighty fine. The girls who work there get top dollar, but don't last long. The madams like to offer variety so there's a big turnover. You don't want that.

"Now look the other way. The farther down this street to the west are the cheaper, dingier houses. They're mostly for sailors, soldiers, and working class men. The women are older and less attractive. Most have been cast out of the more elegant bordellos. Truth be known, that's probably where I'm headed if that sailor of mine don't rescue me pretty soon. You'd do best kind of in the middle, I think."

Star stood up and stretched her arms up high above her head. When she sat back down, she lit a cigarette and offered me one before she continued.

"Yes sir. This Post Office Street really brings in the money to Galveston. If you count up the pimps, madams, cab drivers, household servants, and police who are dependent on prostitution, it becomes clear it is one of this city's major industries. I hear aging girls get one dollar. I get three and that is the going price at the average house. Some places give the sailors a special rate. That's how I met my Harry here. In the fancy houses, you can make up to one hundred dollars for the whole night or ten dollars for fifteen minutes. All the madams get 40% and the girls get 60. The house pays off the bribes, doctor bills, and lawyer fees. If you work at it long and hard and save your money, you can get some ahead. Personally, I don't want to get ahead. I just want to get out of here. You will too one day, is my guess."

"You're right about that. I'll only be doin' this as long as it takes to find me some kind of business to buy and run. My pilot got himself killed so he couldn't come back for me. Hope you have better luck with your sailor."

"Well, the damn war is over so he don't have that excuse, but if I get another offer, I'll sure as hell take it. Ain't no romance in it for me. I am just looking at being old and used up on the Galveston streets. That's my motivation. Not love, for God's sake. You probably loved your pilot, huh?"

"I sure did, but I don't talk none about him no more. Especially now I'm startin' this, ugh, job."

We both laughed at my choice of words. Star stood up and motioned for me to do the same. "Hell. I've read that it is the oldest profession in the world. I like the 'profession' part. Come on in and I'll introduce you to Miss May, the madam. And if I was you, I'd insist on at least five dollars. They'll pay it for you."

Miss May was a cream puff. All ribbons and lace and talcum powder. Fat and funny. I took mental note not to look or act like her if I was ever a madam. A madam? Lord Almighty, is that my plan?

Miss May was all smiles, "Darlin', you are sure a dumpling. Of course you'll get the five dollars you asked for. Men will be falling over themselves to pay it, and if you want to have special customers, we can decide on a higher price for a longer time or a regular time. Now listen up while I explain how it works here and then you can have some supper and a good long sleep. You'll start to work tomorrow."

I had left my suitcase in the wide hall and I was sure glad when Miss May offered me a teacake. Had I eaten all day? Probably not.

Miss May began the instruction like it was rocket

science. She was all business. "Now, when the customer rings the doorbell, the maid answers. He is then shown into the parlor where he can drink, talk, and dance with the girls. You and all the other girls will be dressed in evening dresses and waiting in the dining room. Your workday begins at 4pm and lasts until 2am. You have one week off a month. Naturally, that is when you have your period."

I nodded and hoped I looked like this was all routine for me. It wouldn't do for Miss May to guess I didn't know shit about this fuckin' business.

"The maid will always be sitting here in the hall. She will hand you a clean small towel as you go up the stairs with your customer. First thing you do when you get to your room is collect the money and drop it down to the maid by a string attached to a box. She'll count the money and record your name in the ledger, what time you went upstairs with the customer, and amount of time spent with him. The maid will yell, 'Roll 'em.' That is when you go back into your room to start with your customer. You'll notice all the bedrooms have transoms over the doors that are never closed. The controls are on the outside of the door and the door is never locked. That way everybody can hear what is going on so you don't run the risk of being hurt by some crazy man. Do you have any questions?"

"Yes, I have one. Tell me about the towels."

"The towels are part of my accounting system. At the end of every working day, the towels are collected and counted. The number of towels must match the number of customers beside your name in the ledger. Each of my girls has her own color or pattern. And, of course, you use the towels to clean yourself up, but you know that," she said though a smile.

You have no idea how little I know, was my only thought, as I weakly smiled back.

All of a sudden I was overcome with exhaustion and a heaviness I had never known before. "If I could have a little bite to eat, I'll then get on to sleep. I'm mighty tired from all my travelin'. I just got into Galveston today. Maybe Star can show me around the hotel tomorrow morning."

Miss May laughed as she said, "Sure. Star can do that, but it won't be in the morning. Star, or none of us for that matter, often sees the morning sun. Just hang out in the dining room and she'll find you. And welcome to the Rose Hotel. I'm proud to have you working for me. You certainly are a peach."

My room would be the first one on the right at the head of the wide steps leadin' up to the second floor. I didn't even turn on the light. I stepped in and the hall light was enough to show me the bed. I set my suitcase down, took off my shoes, and laid down on top of the bedspread. After several minutes, I realized I needed to get up and close the door.

As I laid there in the dark, I could hear people in the hotel. The boards in the hall gave notice of folks comin' and goin'. Every once in a while there would be some laughter. I could hear men's voices too. I wasn't afraid, but I wasn't peaceful either.

My sleep, that came and went, was filled with dreams. Not really dreams. More like scenes with me in them.

Me and strangers on top of me. Me and darkness.

Around daylight I finally found the tiny room with the commode. I walked quietly down the empty hall back in my room where I decided to unpack my suitcase.

Actually the bedroom wasn't bad. I loved the deep red plywood walls. On the wall beside a floor lamp hung a fancy framed picture of a large woman with almost nothin' on. Just a thin spread layin' across her middle and nothin' over her fat breasts. The double bed was covered with a right pretty velvet and taffeta spread. The chest of drawers was tall and fancier than most, with a mirror attached to it and plenty of drawers for my few clothes. The light fixture was really something. All crystal and brass. No sir, not a bad room at all.

By the time Star woke up and came to the dining room, I was full up with coffee and all the ham and eggs and hot biscuits I could stuff down. The black cook was willin' to give me seconds. No one else in the whole place was awake but us two.

"There you are," were Star's first words to me when she stumbled into the dining room. "How did you sleep?"

"I made it okay, but it did take me a spell to find the toilet. Maybe you could show me where everything is after you eat?"

"I'll do it but first we will go shopping for you a fancy dress. I'm betting you don't have one." Star was smilin' and friendly even in the mornings. Late morning, that is.

I told the flat out truth, "Don't have one. Never had one. Hope they don't cost much 'cause I ain't got much. I'll wait for you in my room. No need to rush."

I wasn't smilin' as I climbed the stairs up to the second floor of the hotel. What a damn fix I'm in, was my thought as I glanced into my room. Nice furnishings or not, it's what I'll be doin' in here to earn money. No gettin' around it regardless of where I go in my mind while I'm doin' it.

But the only other thing I can do is waitress and look for some man to marry me. I got no education, so I don't know how to do a damn thing. But one thing's for sure, ain't havin' no good man or no bad man ever again. Pain, it's all pain. Pain for what I wanted and pain for what I got.

I'm nowhere near the Edna Arretha Milton I was. No more waitin' and wishin'. I'll do what I have to do to get what I want and I'd best start right now not thinkin' about it too hard.

But it just slipped out anyway. "Bcn, Ben." I moved to the bed and sat down hard.

A few minutes passed before I started talkin' to myself again. "Time to stop blamin' Ben. I ain't his sweetheart no more. And I ain't ever gonna be no one's sweetheart again. It can't be any worse than what it has been, so just stop it and get a backbone. Shit! Ain't nobody bout to kill ya."

I was still sittin' on the bed when Star came bouncin' up the stairs. If she is any indication, I thought to myself, this life won't be so bad. She sure don't act like her soul is shrivelin'.

"Come on, Edna, I'm gonna walk you to the Star Drug Store first. It is a right nice place, and no, it wasn't named for me. The owner, George Clampitt, has made a name for himself here in Galveston. You'll never in your life guess what he has gone and done."

I got up and started for the door. "I'm all ears, Star. What's the guy famous for?" I wasn't really all that interested, but I could act like it.

Star was just bustin' with the news. "Well, that drug store of his has a wonderful soda fountain bar, right in the middle of the big room in a u-shape. The tiles are white with green trim and the bar stools are black. You can order all kinds of sandwiches and ice cream desserts. Hell, it is the best place in town to spend the hot afternoon. The ceilings are high and I 'spec there are at least six ceiling fans going all the time. Mighty pretty too, with wooden blades and upside down white service dishes holding the bulbs. And get this, the lunch counter is desegregated. It is the only place in all of Galveston that niggers can get served."

"Well, that does beat all," I said with appropriate interest.

Star barely took a breath before she continued, "And that ain't all. You'll see on the mezzanine level that Mr. Clampitt has cots available for his customers to lay down on after taking the medicine he gives them. He always keeps an eye on people just in case they have a reaction to the medicine. Now, ain't that something?"

I nodded as we walked along Post Office Street. "He does sound like a right nice fella. Oh, look at that big Coca-Cola sign. I ain't never seen one so big."

We paused in front of the drug store to admire the sign. Then as we stepped through the screen door, cool air from the fans greeted us. I moved away from Star to make my way around the sides of the room where all kinds of products were displayed, along with some jewelry. All kinds of wonderful things to buy.

Carefully I picked up the Pure & Perfect Hunt's Remedy bottle because I wanted to read all about it. The ad was of a young girl in a sailor suit and hat smilin' because of the soothin' skin balm. Another one was really pretty, too. A beautiful lady holdin' a fan asked, 'Don't you want a satin skin?' This skin powder came in four tints: Flesh, White, Pink and Brunet.

I felt a faint stirrin' of enjoyment as I stopped to read the advertisement about Ocean Blue Brand Bath Salts. There was a picture of a happy lady standin' there holdin' a bottle. The sign said, 'As Refreshing As The Ocean Blue.'

I read all the smaller print too: Recommended for the old and the young with advantage and safety. The Tidewater Mineral Springs Company.

By the time I joined Star at the counter, I felt something fresh and light in my body. I took a deep breath and stood up taller. Life in Galveston was going to be so much better than Ventura. Why, I could walk to this drug store every day if I wanted to. No one would care who I was or what I did for my soda money. Maybe I could even buy a pair of those ear bobs.

"There you are. Come sit right here and order something cold. It's on me," Star said as she patted the stool next to her.

In that moment, I felt happy for the first time in a very long while. What luck to have Star as a gal-pal. Without all that makeup, her awful blond hair covered up with a scarf, and just jeans and a plain shirt on, she sure didn't look like no whore.

My smile was honest and my heart not so burdened. A chocolate soda would make my day. No thinkin' about tonight now. No sense in ruinin' the moment with thoughts about what the night would be.

I looked over and said, "Star, tell me what you know about Galveston."

As I took a long swig of the soda, I directed the chitchat away from myself and what I didn't want to think about. I wasn't even conscious of my talent for controllin' conversation because it comes so natural. I did it all the time without even intendin' to.

As I followed Star out the screen door, I thought about how my life had been up to now. There were gonna be some changes. From now on, I would be callin' the shots, and if things were such that I couldn't, well then, I would just up and change whatever it was that had me at the mercy of someone else.

"Well, I don't know much, but I know the important stuff," Star said. "For beginners, if you are a BOI that makes you special."

"What's a BOI?"

"Born on the Island. It gives you an edge. You will see the names John Sealy, who controls the docks and the Moodys, who are the cotton and banking folks. Then of course there are the outside-the-law men like the Maceo family. I know about the two brothers, Rose and Big Sam. Originally they were barbers down at Murdocks on the seawall, but these days they are all over the gambling and prostitution business here in Galveston. You'll hear of some of these places like the Turf Club, the Hollywood Club, and the Balinese Room that's way out over the water. Fancy places to eat and drink and gamble. They say that Vic Fertita is their lieutenant. Ain't likely you'll run across any of these guys because they don't come to the Rose Hotel. Nope, they go to the fancier houses, but just so you know."

"What do you do for fun on your days off?"

Star motioned the direction we should walk. "Of course, that is only one week a month and I always hope my sailor will be in. If we was fancy folks, we'd go to the Grand Opera House, but since we ain't, we go to the beach park and ride the roller coaster. They say it is the roughest one in the whole country and I believe it. I just nearly die every time I ride it. If I was you, I'd wait until I had a date to take me. You need someone to hang onto. It's also fun to ride them hobbyhorses down there. If you grab one of them brass rings as you go by, you get a free ride."

"Might not happen then," I said, with a slight smile. "My datin' days are most likely over."

Star shook her head and said, "At your age? Don't tell me you're throwing in the towel already? Good grief. What you planning on doing with the rest of your life?"

Without hesitatin' I said, "Get ahead. I'm gonna own property and run some kind of business."

"Well, glory be. If that's the case you better get started." Star's laugh was friendly.

As we walked down the street together, Star shook her head. I didn't mind Star's words. Clearly, the woman meant no disrespect. No doubt Star thought my plan sounded too grand to be practical, anyone would. Especially if she knew that my only experience in the sex trade was with Woody. It was time to buy a dress and learn my way around the Rose Hotel. Now my happy feelings were all gone.

Not long after we arrived at the dress shop Star knew about, we found the soft flowing emerald green dress. Every one of the shoppers and Star too, went on and on about how it made my green eyes pop.

I stood a long time starin' in the full-length mirror. I waited for a sense of pleasure or enjoyment or cheer or happiness, but none came. This would be my workin' clothes. Nothing personal. The dress would never be worn outside the Rose Hotel.

That wasn't Edna Arretha Milton in the mirror. No, this unfamiliar person was the reflection of a girl I didn't know. Someone I was in no hurry to know. Maybe, just maybe, I would never have to know.

Back at the hotel there still wasn't much sign of life. A few girls in the dining room eatin' a late lunch weren't much interested in meetin' me. Star headed up the stairs with me followin' slowly. I stopped long enough at my room to leave the package on the bed. Star motioned for me to hurry up.

The hall was a complete square with bedrooms on both sides. The high ceilings helped with the heat, but it still wasn't anywhere near cool. Thank goodness it would be late afternoon before any customers came.

A room way on the other side from mine was just big enough for a deep bathtub and lavatory. One chair in the corner to put your towel and clothes on, so Star said. Then the room right next to it was the toilet. Just one. Star made a joke about havin' to wait in line to crap.

"Seriously though," Star said. "If you have an emergency, Miss May will let you use her private bathroom. See here, she has this whole side of the hall for her apartment. It is really nice. She don't even have to eat with us if she don't feel like it. Everyone likes her because she takes good care of us all. You can bet no awful man gets away with any rough stuff. She walks these halls all night long listening for any foolishness. And you know that your bedroom door can't be locked from the inside. You'll be safe here, Edna. You got nothing to worry about."

"That's good to know," I said. But deep down I believed there was nothin' good about any of this. Stop it, I told myself, don't think about tonight now. Just ask questions.

"Where is the kitchen? Can I go in there to get a drink of water or something out of the icebox if I'm hungry?"

"Sure, that's okay. But you ain't gonna have time to eat at night. And when it gets to be 2am, all you will want to do is go to sleep. I'm telling you, if you don't already know, it takes the starch out of you to have one man after another jabbing at ya."

This was my chance. I needed some idea of what else was in store. So as easy like as I could, I said, "Tell me about any of the extra stuff that I might have to do."

Star sat down at the big kitchen table and looked at me hard and long. For sure she had guessed I didn't know nothin' about this business. But thank goodness, she wasn't gonna let on. I feel stupid and scared to death, and Star knows it. I wonder if she was?

Star explained, "Well, the easy ones are the guys you have for their first time. They usually just want to get it in and shoot off in you without anything else. It gets a little trickier if they become one of your regulars. Then they will want to talk and to feel around on you and they will need you to act as if you really like them. They won't be in such a hurry. You will have to keep it moving so they don't take up too much of your time. But at the same time, you don't want them to realize you want them out the door. Unless they pay up front for extra time, you don't just give it to them."

I sat at that kitchen table with my heart in my throat. My head drooped lower and lower and my eyes finally shut completely. Could I do this? Was there no other way to make a livin'? I was half ready to bolt for the hall when I realized that Star was still talkin'.

"What do you think about this table?"

I wasn't sure I had heard her correctly. "What do you mean? Ain't it just a kitchen table?"

"Yes and no," Star said as she got up and removed the checkered tablecloth.

I got up too and moved away from the bare wooden table. It made no sense, but for some unknown reason I was repulsed by it. The table made my skin crawl even before Star told me why.

One end of it could be propped up and the other end had a hole right in the middle. Star said something about how it was for the blood to flow into a pan on the floor.

"I'm sorry, Edna," Star cried as she struggled to hold

me up. "I didn't mean to scare you so bad. It is just that you need to know that if any of us get pregnant, Miss May has the doctor come here to do it. Naturally he can't have any of us going to his office, but it does make it easier on the girl, too. It ain't a good thing to have happen to you, for sure. I've been lucky so far, but I do know that it can set you back a spell. One girl, a year back, bled to death."

After I could stand on my own, Star poured me a glass of water and suggested it might be a good idea to take a bath and rest up before it was time to go downstairs.

And the bath water did feel good. I even washed my hair and would have sat in the water longer, but my time was up. Star had gone down to the dining room for the big meal of the day, but I couldn't eat a bite. Instead, I shut the bedroom door and lay down on the bed. The other girls laughed and talked now, and that kind of friendly noise helped me relax some. I was startled when Star woke me up to say it was time for the new green dress and all that came with it.

It was a god's blessing I didn't have much time to think about what was happenin'. Miss May had been right. The men made a beeline for me. I would barely get to sit down in the living room before another man would grab me up.

How many was it that first night? Was it twenty or thirty? I had no idea. And thank goodness it didn't take much effort to keep my mind somewhere else. If my life depended on it, I couldn't have described what any of them looked like or how they acted. It was hours of a dream-like existence.

I didn't even have to smile at them. One minute I was returnin' to the living room and the next I was headed back up the stairs. The green dress came on and off easily. The dim light in my bedroom made it possible for the men to not seem too real. They would breathe heavily while I washed them off, and then it didn't take no time for them to come once I lay down on the bed and they got in me. Very few words passed. No emotion shared. Gratitude mumbled as they left.

The best part of the evening was when I got my turn in the bathroom. I douched with strong vinegar before throwin' on a nightgown. Lookin' in the mirror was a mistake I wouldn't make again. The bed felt good without that large soiled towel across the middle of it like it was when I was workin'.

Within a few nights, some of the men wanted more. They were those dreaded repeat customers. Men who had more than five dollars to spend. More money meant more actin'. They wanted a dance or two before goin' upstairs, and then they expected me to act like I knew them and liked them and enjoyed them doin' me.

No way I could escape becomin' a real good fake. I managed to smile and play my part, but how it disgusted me. Not because of the men. No, they were just men with their natural needs. What I hated was the way I was losin' myself, but maybe it was a blessing that I could manage no mental connection with my body. What worried me was that it would take most of the next day to get back to myself and then when I did, there was nothing I welcomed knowin' about Edna Arretha Milton.

My favorite place was Star Drug Store. On afternoons too hot to walk or to take the trolley to the beach, I would sit at the counter and drink a soda. No one more than said hello to me and that was fine by me. Other than Star, I talked to no one.

Instead, I saved all my money, except for what I spent on sodas and vinegar douches. Some day I'd have the money to buy a house and become the madam. Not a high callin', but the only one I could realistically aim for. Yep, me ownin' a whorehouse ain't much of a callin'. It sure ain't a high callin'.

How long would it take me was the question that kept my mind occupied. And how in the world would I ever be able to afford a place on Post Office Street. But I didn't really want to spend the rest of my life in Galveston. It was okay for now, but for some reason I couldn't name, it just didn't feel exactly right.

The weeks turned into months and life at the Rose Hotel was the same, day in and day out. Sleep until noon. Eat a light breakfast and then take a walk to the drug store or around town. Maybe even take a trolley ride to the beach. Eat the main meal at 3pm and be dressed for the night's work by 4. The hours until 2am would be a steady stream of men in and out of me in my bedroom. Sleep was the best part of my existence. The only emotion I experienced was when Star told me that she was leavin'. Without Star, life would be completely solitary.

"Yeah, I ain't waiting on that damn sailor no longer," Star said as she lit another cigarette. "I'll be long gone and married before he even notices."

I felt a sharp stab of hurt and disappointment, but I

tried to not show it. I could act like I didn't care. Hell, I acted all the time. Every damn night of my sorry ass life. Seems like I was actin' more than I was for real.

"Who is the lucky guy? Anyone I know?"

Star was excited to tell. "Oh yeah, you have seen him at the hotel. He has been coming in to see just me since we met a few months ago. He is some older than me, but that don't matter none. What I want is a husband and he has asked if he could be just that. He lives up around Kilgore and owns a small café there. I'll waitress for him and be mighty glad to do it."

"I've waited tables too, in California and it ain't bad work at all. You'll do just fine." I didn't even notice how easily I could now lie without even plannin' on it.

Star went on, "I'm real happy about this, Edna. And the only thing I'll miss is you. Why don't you think about marrying someone and getting out of this trade? You could have your pick of several of them regulars of yours."

"Nope. Nothing doin'. I have my plan and I'll do it one way or the other." I sounded far more sure of myself than I really was. Star just smiled at me a little sadly and that was that.

With Star gone, there was no one I could share my worries with. None of the other girls there at the Rose Hotel were friends. Sure, everyone spoke to everyone at the dinner table, but that was about it. That is, of course, if you weren't mad as a hornet at one of them for takin' too long in the bathtub. Even then, it wasn't my style to cuss 'em out. I really didn't have enough feelings in me to get all that mad.

No. One day was just like the other except for my week off. It was freeing to walk all afternoon long down the seawall, or to sit for hours staring out at the gulf. However, even the breeze and the birds couldn't bring much in the way of sensation. Rentin' a room away from the hotel for that week off would have helped, but that would cost money. I even went back there for the one big meal of the day to save a dime. Ice cream at Star Drug was my only splurge.

Gettin' in and out of a bed with men resulted in me not even experiencin' them as people. And I hated it when they would whine, "Don't you care for me at all?" But I never stumbled at keepin' my distance. Ben was no longer in my mind, but he hadn't left my heart.

Funny how I didn't even get lonesome. But then, one would have to feel human to be lonely and to acknowledge being friendless. I learned pretty quick that the only way I could live my life was to withdraw from it. To act like it wasn't happenin'. Even walkin' down the beach I was never really there. My head stayed in the future.

I took note of how I would do things different from Miss May and what I would copy. I thought about havin' my own home away from the business. My car would be a big aqua-colored one. People would know I was a successful businesswoman and admire me for it. But somehow I couldn't see this happenin' in Galveston. But where? And when?

Worryin' about it wasn't helpin', so I finally got up the courage to ask Miss May for a meetin'. Besides I had something more immediate to confess.

"Now Edna, haven't you been using the oral contraceptive made from Queen Anne's Lace seeds? Didn't you chop the seeds and put them in a glass of water? You know that cutting the seeds releases terpenoids, which blocks progesterone. And you douche with vinegar every night, don't you?" Miss May's wide eyes and anxious voice made it clear that she was upset.

"Yes, sure I have," I hated to tell her, but I did feel a little relief from gettin' the worry off my chest.

"Damn it all to hell, Edna. If you are sure, then there is only one thing to do. I'll call the doctor and he'll be by to take care of you. It won't be an easy thing, but all the girls make it through. Some easier than others."

I knew there was no other remedy, and the memory of those long hours of painful labor hadn't faded much. Too, there was no way I could support a baby and no tellin' who the father was and I wouldn't want to know.

Yet, as I lay in bed that night waitin' for sleep, I couldn't help but feel that if there was a God, this would be one thing He'd never forgive me for.

I'm still goin' in the wrong direction for damn sure. I'm twenty-three years old and my life is a pile of shit. When I get past this abortion, I'm going to talk to Miss May about how I can get out of here and on down the road. There just has to be a way for me to better myself.

Two days later in the morning around 9, I made my way to the kitchen. The horrid table was stripped bare and the one end that could be elevated, was. The doctor and Miss May waited. He took up almost all of the room. What a fat and red and sweaty man. Could he really be a doctor?

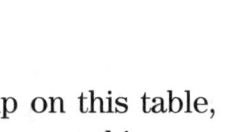

The doctor motioned to me. "Get up on this table, gal, and spread your legs like you done to get this way. I'm gonna tie your ankles to each corner and give you a shot so you won't feel nothing. It'll put you out. We'll get you back to your room and, in a couple of days, you'll be up and about."

I did as I was told and the last thing I remembered was Miss May pattin' my arm and smilin' down at me on that hard table.

Something was wrong. I couldn't get out of bed and the maid was fussin' about all the blood messin' things up. The pain was like a hot fire in my lower belly. Days passed as I lay there in that damp bed, hoping I'd just go ahead and die and get it over with.

"Edna, sit up. You have got to eat something." Miss May sounded tired.

"Is this normal," I mumbled. "Is this the way it goes every time? I don't have the energy to talk, much less eat."

"You are having a bad time of it for sure. That doc ain't much good, but he is the only one I know who will come here when I ask him. You do know it is against the law?"

The only upside to being in bed all week was that it gave me the opportunity to talk to Miss May. Little by little, I learned things were not all that good for her either and hadn't been for some time.

"Edna, this is a risky business and sure not one I'd encourage you to stay in here in Galveston. Since 1949, Police Commissioner Walter Johnston has been the political protector of the prostitution syndicates here.

I read in the paper what he said about the prostitution issue being enveloped in fear and lethargy. It is because Galvestonians want no connection with the outside world. They want this city to remain an isolated island kingdom. But it do look like he is losing ground."

I could now sit up in bed and had the strength to talk. I decided to risk askin', "So are you sayin' that the chances of me gettin' to buy a place here and run it ain't good?"

Miss May nearly fell off the end of the bed. "Are you serious? My lord, girl, you could never earn enough money to pay down on a place along Post Office Street. The only reason I have this hotel is my late uncle, who didn't have no kids of his own, left it to me. And besides it's getting harder and harder to stay open. For a while now, there has been a community surveillance of Post Office Street to produce evidence for a grand jury hearing, so keeping my doors open is no longer a piece of cake. Prostitutes are being shifted around to avoid detection and it boils down to an endurance contest. There's the 'controlled sex' group and their opponents who preach that 'to control is to condone'."

When I didn't respond, Miss May took a deep breath and finished with, "Our Mayor Herbert Cartwright has recommended to the Texas Legislature that prostitution, liquor by the drink, and gambling be regulated. He says the people of Galveston have more or less accepted it and really ought to be commended for not being hypocrites. Yes sir, I like that man. I have voted for him every time."

I took in every word. Secret whispers from my bones

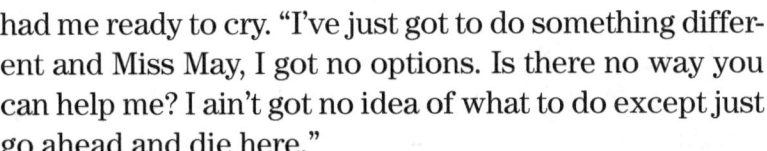

had me ready to cry. "I've just got to do something different and Miss May, I got no options. Is there no way you can help me? I ain't got no idea of what to do except just go ahead and die here."

Miss May took her time standing up. "Let me think about it, Edna. There just might be a way out of here for you. Maybe Jessie Williams could use you. She has a place in the country near a town called La Grange. Ain't nothing like Post Office Street. I understand she has a few acres with a big old farmhouse on it. Country living and country folks. I'm told that boys from Texas A&M and even some state government men make it down there. Now I think about it, Jessie is getting on up in years, too. Might just be that you could buy the place off her after a spell."

I was already feelin' better, and then a couple of days later when Miss May told me she had talked to Jessie Williams and she had said I should come on and take a bus to LaGrange, I smiled for the first time in weeks.

Here was my chance. Somehow I just knew that one day I'd buy Jessie's house called the Chicken Ranch and be the businesswoman I had always dreamed I'd be. I had enough money for the bus ticket and I'd leave tomorrow. Wasn't up to workin' yet and there was no good reason to wait. Besides, Miss May needed my bedroom 'cause I sure hadn't made her no money now in weeks.

The Kerrville Bus Station was at the Eckel's Sweet Shop and, as I stepped off that bus, I stood up tall. I wasn't going to be whorin' for one minute longer than I had to, and in the meantime I was gonna think of myself as a businesswoman. I'd work hard and save every dime

I could.

I smiled at the bus driver when he handed me my ole suitcase and my heart was light as I walked toward the courthouse that stood in the middle of downtown La Grange. It wasn't lunchtime yet so I decided to go into the courthouse just to see what it looked like on the inside. There were four doors, one on each side of the building. I stopped to read the description framed on the wall inside the door I went in. I learned it was Romanesque Revival style of architecture, whatever in the hell that was. The plaque read that the exterior walls were built of blue Muldoon sandstone and trimmed with red Pecos sandstone, pink Burnet granite and white Belton limestone. It was three stories high and was mighty fine, and silly as it was, I felt proud.

The buildings around the courthouse looked like some of them in Galveston. The Hermes Building was built in 1939 and another building stood on the opposite side of the square with the same name. A building on the east side named Vallejo was built in 1855 and across from it was another one with the same name, but no date.

Those must be important people in LaGrange, I decided as I made my way toward one of the meat markets on the north side of the square. I chose Prause Meat Market. "A Family Tradition Since the 1890's" the sign read. At the entrance was a newspaper stand so I bought the local paper, *The Fayette County Record*, Tuesday, 1952.

While I ate some BBQ pork with a slice of white bread, white onions, and dill pickles on butcher paper,

I sat right there and read that local paper like I was already a part of the town. This La Grange was gonna be my home so I started right in on learnin' about it. The paper was the first one of the new year, 1952, and on the front page was a story about the sheriff's final report of 1951.

Fewer Traffic Deaths Urged in '52
This is the last report for the year 1951, and the holidays are over for a while and everyone is trying to settle down and get the new year started off

Except for the war troubles in Korea, 1951 was a good year. We in the sheriff's department have a lot to be thankful for, both personally and officially. Our health was good and everyone was real nice to us during Christmas and we did not have too much work to do. We enjoyed staying at home with our families and not being called out too often. One thing we were especially thankful for was that we did not have any more traffic accident deaths during the holidays. The year ended with the death total still eight which was the same number killed each year for the past three years. I certainly hope we can get through the year 1952 with a lot less traffic deaths.

I wasn't interested in the list of arrests so I started reading another front-page story.

La Grange Becomes Polio Conscious. Two Cases Rumored; One Probable
La Grange and vicinity became polio conscious last week as reports got out that two local people had been stricken. One case has since been diagnosed as probable

polio while the other proved to be a spinal infection.

The probable polio victim is 25 year-old George J Prilop, father of three small children – the oldest 3 years and the youngest two weeks old – who is now in the polio ward of Jefferson Davis hospital in Houston.

Mr. Prilop became ill while on his job at Farmers Lumber Company here on December 31. After being hospitalized here, he was taken by Koenig ambulance to Houston.

His wife, Mrs. Delores Janda Prilop, father, George H. Prilop and Miss Ann Janda, visited the hospital Sunday and reported that the patient's condition is very serious. While not positively diagnosed as such, the illness is believed to be polio of a severe but non-crippling variety.

Present with the patient are his mother, who accompanied him to Houston, and a sister, Mrs. Carl Frazier, Jr., a registered nurse, employed at the Veterans Hospital in Houston.

The other case first suspected as possible polio was that of Richard Von Minden, 6-year-old son of Mr. and Mrs. Clinton Von Minden. His father, employee of the A&P Store here, reported Monday that, although the youngster was still in the hospital, he was well on the way to recovery.

Right this minute there ain't one soul on this earth who could care for me if I got polio, I thought, as I took another bite of the really tasty meat. I looked around the crowded room at the locals and ventured a smile at one old lady. I wonder if I stay here long enough if that will change. If I buy this here Chicken Ranch and become an independent businesswoman, will that get me friends? Might there be someone or maybe even several people in this LaGrange that might care about me? They wouldn't care one little bit that I owned a whorehouse?

Lordy, that ain't likely and I know it. So I turned the page to read the Cozy Theatre movie ads. At least I'll get to take in a movie the week I'm off work. The last time I saw one was with Ben in Ventura.

To get away from that memory as fast as I could I read the list of comin' attractions:

Meet Me After The Show with Betty Grable and Eddie Albert. *Callaway Went That away* with Fred MacMurray, Dorothy McGuire, Howard Keel. *Cattle Drive* with Joel McCrea and Chill Wills. *Half Angel* with Joseph Cotton and Loretta Young.

As I finished eatin', one more story got my attention. I had never owned a car and didn't even know how to drive, but after I was a businesswoman, I would buy me an aqua one. Might be a Plymouth.

New Plymouth Makes Debut Here Friday In Super Fashion The new Plymouth automobile for 1952 went on display here Friday, Jan. 4 in the showroom of the Meiners Motor Company, local dealer. Shown to the scores of admirers was Plymouth's Cranbrook four-door sedan which, according to E.W. Meiners, local dealer, is one of the Plymouth line of cars that is 'a more beautiful, smoother operating, easier riding, safer car which features 46 important improvements; there is new beauty in the car's road-hugging, sweeping appearance, and color harmony perfection in the new interiors.'

The new car, according to Mr. Meiners, has been improved to provide 'the most gentle ride, the smoothest engine performance, and the greatest safety ever built into a car for the low price field.' LaGrange's local dealer cordially invites the inspection of the general public to the new Plymouth, feeling confident that it will merit the approval of all who seek an automobile in this price range.

Oh, they have dances here abouts. I also knew before I even read the ad that I wouldn't never get to go. No socializin' with the locals was a rule regardless of where you were workin'. But I read it anyway:

Dance – Tietjen Hall on Saturday, Jan. 12, 1952. Music by Bobby Marek's Orch. Admission: Gents 36 cents. Ladies 36 cents. Tax Included. Everybody is welcome.

Well, not really. I folded up the paper and stood up. Better get a move on. No tellin' how far it is to the Chicken Ranch, but I'm bound to walk it. Sure as hell not gonna ask anyone in here for directions.

Nevertheless, probably an hour later as I walked north out of town like Miss May said, I decided to risk asking the teenager on the bicycle where it was.

"You ain't there yet, lady. Keep goin' straight yonder and pass over the highway. Then it'll be on your right after a curve in the dirt road. You'll get there before dark if you keep movin'."

By the time I turned off the dirt road to the white frame house between the trees, the lunch at Prause's was long gone. Not only was I hungry, but bein' still weak, the old suitcase felt like it weighed a ton. But I could and would act real perky for Miss Jessie. First impressions are important. Everybody knows that.

"You that gal from Galveston?" the black woman asked as she opened the screen door.

I noticed it had no latch or handle on the outside. "Yes, I am. My name is Edna Milton and I'm here to see Miss Jessie."

"Fine. You can take yo'self on back to her office. Go straight on past the dining room and you'll see it. She is 'specking you, honey."

I looked straight ahead, payin' no mind to the room except to note it was empty. The smells from the kitchen made my stomach catch. Thank goodness I hadn't missed supper. At the door I set my suitcase down and called out, "Miss Jessie?"

"Come in, Edna, and take a load off. We'll be having dinner in a few minutes and I bet you're hungry."

Jessie Williams was not a Miss May. Tall, lean, with knowin' eyes in a face that no longer held any hint of beauty. Her voice was civil and her manner cordial, so why did I feel exposed?

"Yes, ma'am, I sure am. Walkin' from town took some doin'." But right away I added with a smile, "This sure is pretty country. Never seen so many big trees. The town is nice, too."

First impressions, I remembered.

Jessie made no bones about lookin' me up and down before decidin' to go with the subject I had chosen. "It is that. They tell me originally this area was a large Indian camping ground only to be one of the top choices for the capital city of the new Republic of Texas some fifty years later. Missed it when President Sam Houston vetoed the bill. The name, La Grange, is right pretty, too. In French it means 'the meadow.' It was founded by Colonel John H. Moore, an Indian fighter and hero of the Texas Revolution. Settlers from Tennessee who came in the 1820's named it. I've called it home since 1905 when I bought a small house along the banks of the Lower Colorado River and opened a brothel. Didn't take me too long to realize I needed to be outside the city limits, so in 1915, me and Grace Koplan bought this 11 acres with a small house on it for 700 dollars. Those were the days when you could pay only 100 down and 25 a month. It took me till 1917 to pay it off. Then in 1920 Grace married and moved to Wichita Falls. I bought her half for 1200 and it's been my baby ever goddamn day since."

I took in every word, especially the last three. Am I gonna feel like that one day? was the quick thought I had before respondin' to Jessie's history lesson.

"I've never really had a feelin' of home anywhere. My folks moved from pillar to post in Oklahoma and those years in Ventura was one room in a boardin' house. And the hotel at Miss May's was nice, but it weren't no home."

I sat in silence for a minute. Lookin' straight at Miss Jessie I continued, "I'm sure countin' on stayin' here and makin' a go of it. I'll work right hard for you and be no trouble at all. I'm sure Miss May told you about the abortion that went really bad. For sure I won't be gettin' pregnant ever again."

With no show of emotion or interest, Jessie said, "And that's a blessing in this business. I'll give you a week, Edna, to see how you fit. I run a tight ship, the girls will tell ya, but no one around here ever gets hurt. You'll learn my rules tomorrow afternoon before you go to work. Your bedroom is yours to decorate any way you please. One week off a month and your pay will depend on each job, but you know that."

Jessie nodded towards the door as she stood up painfully, and I realized Miss May was right about her being sick with arthritis. I was glad to hear her say with a weary smile, "I hope you work out, Edna, I really do. My place here in the country beats the hell out of Post Office Street in Galveston, but by now you know that happiness is for four year olds."

Jessie's eyes narrowed just a little. "Make sure you have that smile on your face for the customers. Remember they are here to buy a few minutes of pleasure. Now, go get yourself something to eat and then Della will show you your room. Rest up and I'll talk to you some more tomorrow afternoon before dinner at six."

The dining room was now full of girls talkin' and laughin'. Jessie didn't move to follow me in so I took the bull by the horns and with the best smile I could muster announced my presence with a "Hi, ya'll. I'm Edna Milton. Just off the boat from Galveston and I've never been so hungry."

It was the right thing to say. They all stopped their visitin' to speak to me, laugh, and offer me a chair. I looked around at the young attractive faces and the many big bowls of fried chicken, mashed potatoes, corn on the cob, sliced tomatoes, cornbread, and homemade pickles on the large oval table. I would have to use extra control not to gobble my food down.

The talk was familiar and Maizie, the plump blond seated next to me, asked about life in Galveston. Between bites, I made Galveston sound like the ultimate in adventure, but I was careful to add that I sure was ready for some country living.

Della was ready to show me to the bedroom the minute I took my last bite of apple cobbler. The black woman was at least six feet tall with shoulders like a man's and eyes that didn't blink in a strong face.

I snatched up my suitcase and followed her down a long hall that turned this way and that. At the door Della paused and for the first time spoke to me.

"Now Edna, this here is yo room. The nearest bathroom is on down this hall to the right. Help yo'self to a bath and be to home. Like Miss Jessie said, you can move the furniture to suit ya and decorate any way you fancy. I'd wait till after next week though, if I was you."

I stepped into the room with the thought already formin' in my mind. No decoratin' or movin' furniture. This room will look just like it does this minute the day I leave it for the last time. Nothin' of me will ever be in here. My clothes will have to hang in the closet, and I'll burn them when I leave. This is not my home. It is where I work. I'll look at it tomorrow. All I have the strength to do now is get a bath and to bed. I've got to be strong enough to start work tomorrow evening.

I couldn't wake up. The sun came in the window. I felt it rather than saw it. Again and again I would drift off, only to try to rouse out of a stupor, but not be able to move. Am I dead? I don't feel bad, but I can't move.

For how long this dreamlike morning lasted there was no way to know. Finally I was able to turn over and raise up to see the Early American dresser across from the bed. It was old and scratched and the bedside table wasn't much better. The lamp on it was lopsided. The chenille bedspread was clean but no longer a true green. The maple headboard to the double bed was plain and old. A washstand with a simple small mirror over it stood in a corner next to the only window. The curtains were a cotton print of sunflowers. The only chair in the room was a wooden rocker with a bright green cushion.

My feet hit a wood floor that needed polishin'. Everything was clean but much more basic than at Miss May's. The door opened easily and quietly so I could weave my way to the bathroom. Country livin'!

After a few minutes I had unpacked my suitcase and stored it in the closet. I threw on some jeans and covered my sweatshirt with my only jacket. Coffee was available in the dining room but no one else was yet awake. The coffee was hot and really good.

I took my large cup and walked out the front door. The late morning was sunny and bright. I looked up at the blue cloudless sky and then to the trees where the birds were singin'. As I walked around the house and away towards the woods, I felt alive and strong. I wasn't smilin', but my soul almost was. I took a few steps and then stopped to listen to nature all around me. A squirrel up a tree. A rabbit starin' me down. How long had it been since I was out in woods? Certainly not in Ventura or Galveston. God it felt good just to breathe.

Was that Della callin'? Maybe it was time to eat again.

From the kitchen came huge hot biscuits, eggs with ham, blackberry jam and butter and a big pot of coffee. Within minutes Miss Jessie was holdin' court. Seems breakfast was a time for the madam to review the rules by tellin' a story that made a point of them. Everyone ate and listened.

"Some years back a delightful young girl from Alabama came to work for me here. I'm telling you, it didn't take her no time to become a major attraction. I liked her and so did all the other girls here. Della even liked her. Didn't you, Della?"

This brought laughter from around the table. I ventured a smile.

"Dark clouds began appearing on the horizon, however, when the son of a prominent citizen began showing her too much attention. Then you know what? This pretty young thing made a major mistake when she insisted that her private life was her own and returned his affection. It wasn't long before the two of them started going together to various public places and I got word that there was talk of a real raid and a permanent shut-down."

Jessie paused for emphasis before she continued more slowly, "I hated to do it, but it didn't take me but a New York minute to send her packing. Word was she suddenly had a sick mama in Alabama to tend to. Nobody has ever seen her sweet ass in Texas since."

Silence fell in the dining room and it took Miss Jessie a full minute before she turned to Maizie to ask, "And the moral of that there story is?"

Maizie turned red, put down her coffee cup, and answered in a small voice, "The rule is that no one who works here can have a relationship with any man or boy in La Grange or surrounding towns. It stirs up the women folks and that ain't good for business."

"And that's an easy one for you, ain't it, Maizie, being that you're married?"

I couldn't help myself. I stared at Maizie in amazement. Why in holy hell would any woman work here if she had a husband? It made me boilin' mad.

Maizie lowered her eyes and voice as she murmured, "Yes'um."

"Edna! I'll talk to you after breakfast instead of later today. Come on into my office when you're done. I'll be in there working on my books."

This change of plans suited me just fine. I jumped up to make it to the bathroom before the others and to stop by my room to brush my teeth. Maizie still sat with her head down, but I didn't stop to talk to her. Later, I needed to learn about everyone in this place, and I'd start with Maizie. Whorin' for a husband. Shit! That'll be the day.

As soon as I sat down in Jessie's office, she started, "Edna, May told me you are a right smart girl and one I don't have to watch like a hawk. That's good to know and I'm depending on it. I'm sure you know by now that the most money is the 'four-gets'."

I responded immediately, "Yes, ma'am. Get up. Get on. Get off. Get out. It's the regulars that make it more work. You have to listen to them; act like you like them, and leave them feelin' they are the best thing you ever had between your legs. Takes more puttin'-on than I fancy, but I sure can do it."

Then I smiled confidently and continued, "Like I said, Miss Jessie, I'm plannin' on stayin' here and workin' real hard. No need for you to worry none about me."

Jessie nodded, "Fine. Fine. The pay is from three dollars up to forty based on the time spent. I let my girls collect the money as soon as they get in the room, for a quick date or around the world. Now I know I don't need to tell you your business, but there is one thing you should know. I don't hold with none of that trashy French whore stuff here at my place. Those soldiers back from the war got another think coming if they want my girls to go beyond the usual missionary position. I am up and down the hall all night long and if I hear any thing that tells me it's going on, I'll be in your room with my rod. I won't hit you a lick, but that man will be leaving without his pants. Remember, too, there ain't no doors locked here and I'm in charge. You have a problem with any of that, Edna?"

"Absolutely not, Miss Jessie. I'm in agreement with you. I'm thinkin' there's a right way and a wrong way to do everything."

"Good. Good. Now I hope you have a nice cocktail dress. Nothing too skimpy, but pretty."

"I do have one, but I'll be getting me a new one soon as I can."

"All right. Dinner is at 6pm. You can dress right after. Most don't come until dark. Those that come earlier are regulars and we know who is to be ready for them. I'm thinking that it won't take long for you to have regulars.

You are a mighty fine looking gal. Good thing you want to work plenty. Like in Galveston, you will work three weeks out of each month, staying at the Ranch the whole time. At Easter, Thanksgiving, and Christmas, there will be holiday meals. The girls like to have a Christmas tree and we draw names to exchange gifts. What you do with your week off is up to you. Most of the girls leave for a change of scene."

I could tell that Jessie had delivered this speech many times and her eyes told me that she was tired to death of it. If she took any pride in bein' a businesswoman, there sure weren't no seein' it.

"Oh yeah, there is one last thing. I don't allow no banking in LaGrange. Can't have no one knowing our business out here. Keep it in a sock; bury it someplace around the house, or whatever. Just don't open no bank account in town."

I left the office and headed outside again. I wanted to walk off my breakfast and enjoy the cool winter day some more. Thank goodness I didn't have to go on the road. With eleven acres around the house, I could walk and walk. The solitude of the woods and the cool breeze on my unpainted cheek refreshed me. Work didn't come to mind at all. That was the best part.

Night came and with it the Galveston green dress. I applied the Max Factor makeup from Star Drug Store and brushed back my freshly washed, long reddish brown hair, and then clipped it with my only fancy hairpin.

Once Della let the customer in—after she was sure he was sober and of age—a bell rang in the den in the back of the house to let us girls know we must come out to be on display. I filed out with everyone else and sat down in the large waiting room. The black chairs with ashtrays beside each lined the walls. The carpet was green with flowers just like the curtains.

Actually, I decided as I sat down, this room is awful. There was a small space to dance and a jukebox and coke machine on one end. I sat down to chat with a smile on my painted face. Like at Miss May's, a dance or two might happen next. And, like at Miss May's, I was grabbed up first thing. I led the way to my bedroom. I was back at it. He wanted a quick date and paid me.

His hands were already on me. "What's your name, little lady? I'm Travis from Austin. In the government there." His voice sounded boastful.

"Oh how excitin'. Tell me what you do there, Travis." I smiled at him as I unzipped my dress and let one shoulder fall down. I moved my hips slowly as it fell to the floor. Then I slipped out of my bra and panties. He was starin' at me the whole time. I motioned him to the washbowl in the corner. I strolled over to it in the nude so by the time Travis had his pants off and I was washin' his fat dick with slow long strokes, he was red-faced and gaspin'.

"Hell, I'm not sure I can make it past the washing," the man whined.

"Oh, sure you will. A big strong guy like you will be mighty good." I smiled while thinkin', that's my plan, mister, 'cause you've paid for me whether you get it or not.

He barely made it to the bed before he came. As I patted his arm and looked disappointed, I could tell he was not a happy customer. His large eyes were narrowed and his mouth was twisted up in a sour knot. Instantly I went to work on his ego.

"Now Travis, honey. Don't you fret. You came so fast because you are so good. I can tell you that lots of men have trouble gettin' it up. You should be proud, and when you come back, I hope you will want me again because I sure do want you to come in me."

As he left my bedroom, he assured me he would be back next week and I was glad to see he was all smiles. After he shut the door, I pulled on my dress thinkin', since I already know I'm goin' to hell, lyin' like a dog don't matter none at all.

And so it went, night after night, week after week. Somehow the men at the Chicken Ranch seemed a leg up on the Galveston bunch. The young Aggies from A&M hardly ever made it past the washin' until they got smart and started stoppin' at the gas station outside of Giddings to jack off first.

The local men had their regulars and usually arrived at odd hours. Naturally they wanted to talk about their lives and it was my job to make sure they didn't get too attached. When I saw that was happenin', I'd tell Miss Jessie and she would then steer them to some other girl.

Then there were those government types from Austin. Full of self-importance and bullshit, like all their kind. But, no bad guys. Della had a nose for trouble and they didn't get past her. I don't know what Miss Jessie paid her, but she was worth every penny.

We got to go to town on Saturday afternoons. Nice conservative slacks or skirts and no bare legs. We had to stay together to shop and Miss Jessie's last words to us as we were gettin' in the car was always, "Now don't say or do nothing that brings attention to yourselves. You act like respectable country ladies."

Her warning always hit me wrong. Was she sayin' I wasn't a lady? That bedroom didn't define me, but then who would know that?

What to do on my week off was my only problem. In Galveston there was no end of free things to do, but La Grange wasn't a tourist town and it wouldn't do for me to be seen around the square too often. So I'd take my long walks and go on down the dirt road for a ways. I enjoyed readin' the library books I'd get on Saturdays when we went to town because I was gettin' better at it. I'd just stay in my room at night and be glad I was alone.

Savin' my money was the important thing. I had to be ready the minute Miss Jessie was. My plan was the same: to own the Chicken Ranch; buy a house in La Grange, and be a successful businesswoman.

Maizie was my favorite working girl. She was nothin' like Star, but I liked talkin' to her. On her week off, she went home to Yoakum where her husband lived. It didn't take me long to get to that subject–a husband. Shit!

"Maizie, tell me about your husband," I said one hot afternoon when we sat out under the trees tryin' to stay cool.

"Nothing to tell. Why do you ask?" Her head had dropped again as was her habit when she was uncomfortable with the topic of conversation.

"Oh, I don't know. I guess it is mainly because I don't understand you workin' here if you have a husband."

"He ain't much of a husband and never was. Old Bernard is up in his 70's now; his kids are all grown and gone so he didn't need me around the house cooking and cleaning as much. You see, I was only fifteen when we married. I didn't have no say in it."

I felt a pain of recognition. "Hell, that's what happened to me, too, only I was sixteen. My brother married me off to a jerk friend of his. Who done it to you?"

Maizie perked up. With my past being like hers, she didn't mind tellin' the whole story. "Oh my folks were always moving from one town to another. My dad did odd jobs and my mom worked in cafés. There were too many of us, so when I got grown, Bernard, one of mom's customers, noticed me and asked if he could take me off their hands. He was old then with a wife in the grave and a house full of kids to tend. He didn't want to sleep with me. I guess he was too old for that and more kids was the last thing he wanted. So I just took care of his house and family until they all left. He sits at home now on his small farm and likes having me to talk to when I'm home a week."

"And how do you feel about that?" As I waited for Maizie's reply, I wondered, where is your ambition, girl?

Maizie looked at me like she had never thought about it before. I could tell that no one had ever paid her much mind. It took her a few minutes to think what to answer.

"I don't rightly like it. Not because Bernard is ugly to me. He ain't and never has been. It's just that he is so boring. He got nothing to talk about. Would you believe all he can think to say to me is what went in the garbage since I been gone. All he does is work the fields and watch TV at night. And the thing is, I won't even get his house and land when he's gone. It goes to his kids."

"Well, why don't you change your life, Maizie? Ain't no law sayin' you have to keep goin' back to that house and old man. How old are you anyway?"

"I'll be 21 next month. What you got in mind?"

I laughed. "I ain't got nothin' in mind. It ain't my life. But you can bet your last dollar I have something in mind for mine. All it takes is the desire and money and time. I got two of those and am workin' on the third."

Maizie dropped her head and was silent.

I let it be for a few minutes, and then said, "Why don't you just start thinkin' about what you would like to do to make money and live independent of any man. We can then talk about it and I'll help you all I can. Bernard can't know how much you make. You could start keepin' some back for your plan so that when you had enough and knew which way to go–you could git."

Maizie's eyes were full of tears and it hurt my heart to see it. Nevertheless, I couldn't stop myself from thinkin' how could anyone be so dumb. And along with that thought came a feelin' of superiority and it felt mighty good. Now I had Maizie's life, not just mine, to manage.

I gave her a warm hug and said with authority, "Now don't you shed any more tears. Get up and get excited about what you can make of yourself. Bein' a whore ain't a life callin'. It's a sorry way to what you want to be. Start thinkin' about it and we'll put our heads together and figure it out for you. Yes ma'am, Miss Maizie, I want to see your backside headin' down that road to Bernard for the last time. Come on now. Let's go get us some lemonade."

Eventually Miss Jessie got around to askin' me what the breakfast story moral was. She loved her stories and the girls dreaded them, but I found them all interesting. Not every morning, but at least once or twice a month Jessie held court.

"Have I ever told y'all about Tolita, that Mexican girl from Presidio, Texas? Hell, she was the most popular girl here for over three months a few years back. Yes sir, she was a dark beauty like I'd never seen before or after, and the men couldn't get enough of her. Her desire to satisfy every customer to the max was unbelievable. And there were times when she would jump up and start wildly dancing and that added spice to her attractiveness.

"But then there were those times during the evening when her bursts of anger, spiked with loud cursing in bastardized Spanish-English would startle the victims of these outbursts, and everybody would run for cover. Some of the men told me about how she would act after they got done. They told me she kept a small crucifix in her room and she would kneel down and ask forgiveness before putting her clothes back on."

Every one of us around the breakfast table, includin' me, stopped eatin' and looked flabbergasted.

"Naturally she had a story, and when men would ask what a nice girl like her was doing in a place like this, she would tell them about life in Presidio. Her breasts had developed to their present large size by the time she was twelve years old. Her father, a sometimes-construction worker more concerned about her four younger brothers, encouraged her to associate with men in their late-teens and early twenties. Because of the prestige involved in early marriages, she was more than happy to oblige.

"So by the time she was thirteen she was pregnant. She was uncertain about who the father was. Her own father kicked her out of his house. The last thing he needed was another mouth to feed. All Tolita could do was hitchhike to Houston, where she worked as a dishwasher in a Mexican restaurant until she miscarried three months later. She was fired from her job because she got an infection and missed too much work. She couldn't pay her rent, so a young Anglo she had met at the bus station agreed to give her a place to stay. Within a few weeks she was on the streets supporting him until she heard of the Chicken Ranch and showed up here on my doorsteps. She didn't last because girls like Tolita are the greatest danger to me. You're on, Edna."

I could tell Miss Jessie was expectin' something special out of my mouth. So I looked straight at her and said with a smirk, "What we do to make money is a sin."

After a group gasp, all the girls stared at me in amazement, but Jessie was not put out. She laughed in a light-hearted way. "Edna, you are a good 'un. Now tell us what you really think."

"It don't take much smarts to know that, like Tolita, we all have our stories. Bein' a whore ain't on the list of possible career options with a great future. Some misfortune got us here. But our stories don't have to do us in like it did her. Seems to me, Tolita's idea of herself was that she was a whore. She expected God to forgive her, but she couldn't forgive herself. If you carry bad thoughts about yourself around day in and day out, it will make you crazy. That is what happened to her. She couldn't keep a lid on the pain in her head. She must not have been workin' towards something else. She needed to have a place to put her mind besides that bed."

"And it is bad for business because?" Jessie would have her answer.

I stood up and took one last sip of coffee. "Men come here to find some pleasure. We are paid to provide it. When our own demons get us down, that makes us unpredictable and cause for Miss Jessie to worry."

No one person at that table, including Jessie, said a word, and as I left the silent dining room, I felt something new. It followed me out the door and into the woods.

Power! For the first time ever I felt powerful. I would make a good leader. I could influence people. "I think I'm proud of myself," I said out loud to no one.

And so it went, year after year. I got to where I could 'work' in my sleep. Seldom was there any excitement. Always there was the routine: sleep till noon; eat a hearty breakfast; take long walks around the eleven acres; read or watch TV in the afternoons; after dinner the party dress, the makeup on; the steady stream of men waiting for my complimentary words and available warm body.

Seldom did I dream of Ben, but when I did, it was always the same one: Ben is sittin' on his horse with his hand held out to me. He smiles and says, "Come on, gal. I'm awaitin' fer ya."

After havin' this dream, I could count on the next day

being a downer. Nevertheless, time rolled on. Little by little, Jessie allowed me to help her and she took time to fill me in on how the business worked and who the important players were. And of course, those breakfast stories of Jessie's continued as a tradition.

Her most recent was, "In the spring of 1917, two freckle-faced young pixies arrived at my doorstep. They were not the first to seek shelter and employment at my then three-room house, but they were the first to be allowed to stay. Shortly after the Armistice of 1918, one of the sisterly pair fell in love with one of her out-of-town customers. He was an older man, charming, educated, and wealthy, and while there is no evidence he was the originator of the well-worn phrase, 'Let me take you away from all this,' he must have chosen words to that effect. The two were married and lived together in a stately old mansion in San Antonio until the old gentleman's death more than thirty years later."

Jessie smiled as she looked around the breakfast table for her victim. She went past me and then circled back. "Okay, Edna, what can you do with that?"

I could tell Jessie loved this part. Without hesitatin', I said, "We can only fall in love with a man from at least a hundred miles away. Any local is off limits."

All the girls laughed and agreed. Everyone knew not to hold her breath for such a development. And I was still glad I didn't want to depend on a man for the life I wanted. As Jessie moved slowly away from the table in her wheel chair, I knew it couldn't be too much longer.

More and more often now during the afternoons, Jessie took the time to tell me about her experiences in

LaGrange. We both were aware I would buy the Chicken Ranch, but nothing was actually said. Didn't need to be.

"Edna, since 1915 when I bought this place, I have always had an alliance with the Sheriff of Fayette County. I remember August Loessin and his brother, Will, who was chief deputy as well as city marshal. Those were fine men and I stayed on good terms with them. Back then, the sheriff visited every evening to pick up gossip and get information on criminals who had done some bragging to the girls. I saw to it that this place of mine caused the law no trouble or embarrassment, and the law repaid me by ignoring my existence. As transportation got better, more and more politicians and lawmen felt welcome and comfortable to come here. Business was so good that I started adding rooms for the growing number of girls working here. Yep, it has been a money-making business for me and if I wasn't getting so damn old, I'd still be good at it."

"You never had no hard times?" I said.

"Hell, yes, I had hard times. Like everybody else in business when the stock market crashed in 1929, there were fewer customers with less to spend, and there were more girls wanting to work for me. By 1932 the price for a regular date was down to $1.50, but that didn't help much. Few men had cash and even fewer were willing to part with it. So I had to change from a cash basis to what I called 'a poultry standard.' One chicken for one date. It was a good move because I could appear on the tax roll as a chicken farm. Looking legal is always important."

I laughed. "And I bet, with all those chickens, the

girls never went hungry."

"No, no, they damn sure didn't. And I also made certain LaGrange looked the other way by giving money to local civic clubs and church bazaars. My girls never got involved with local men, and whenever they were out in town, they looked and acted like any other young ladies. I made sure of that. Yes, yes, I did."

Jessie stretched her frail body in her wheelchair and finished with a show of pride. "I think I done all right by everybody. My girls shopped in town; they got weekly medical checkups I paid for; I bought groceries from local merchants on a rotating basis, and the Ranch had the reputation for discipline, cleanliness, and discretion."

"After the war, I guess business picked up." I wanted to know everything about the history of my business-to-be. "If you ain't too tired and have time tell me more."

"Lord, I say it did." Jessie slapped her lap and laughed out loud. "By the 1940's every brothel from Maine to Malibu had its resident college graduate and there were many from the University of Texas. These co-eds financed an education by working at the Chicken Ranch during the summer breaks. When classes started in the fall, the co-eds would return to Austin and their studies. They lived in swanky apartments, drove new cars, and wore the latest fashions. Sometimes male students from LaGrange would see them in class but nothing was ever said. And these college co-eds weren't the only ones paying for an education with earnings from the Chicken Ranch. No sir, many a prominent businessman can thank his sweet wife for the education she earned for him by working for me. While hubby was busy with his classes at the University of Texas, the wife was entertaining the Aggies. I do believe it was during the 1940's that the Chicken Ranch became an initiation. If you wanted to be an Aggie, you had to participate in the tradition."

I hoped Jessie didn't notice how mad this made me. For damn sure I would put an end to this. The very idea. Young college girls and wives of students workin' here. No, they won't. Only girls who don't have no other options will work at my Chicken Ranch. Whorin' ain't no summer time thing to do for fun money, and it sure ain't for helpin' no man get an education or nothin' else for that matter. Spreadin' your legs should only be a last resort for uneducated women. Do it and get out as soon as you can. I'm gonna see to it. Having authority over college girls and wives would be tricky, and I ain't takin' it on. Nope. For sure not. The gals here will be workin' for me cause they have to. Period.

I had arrived at the Ranch at the right time. The fifties was the decade remembered for absolutely nothing, except maybe the comin' of Elvis Presley, but it was the heyday for life at the Chicken Ranch. Business boomed.

I worked hard and saved my money. Seldom was there enough trouble to even talk about; however, in January of 1958, the sheriff and Deputy Charlie Prilop answered a call from the Chicken Ranch about a robbery in progress. They arrived to find one man stuffin' money in a pillowcase while another held a gun over several women tied up in the next room.

In the early part of November 1961, we started talkin'

about me buyin' Jessie out. By now Jessie was very tired and confined to her wheelchair. I was past tired of whorin' and I had earned enough money to buy the Ranch.

"Jessie, tell me what I don't know about Sheriff Jim." I poured myself another cup of coffee in the hopes it would warm me up. It was cold as rip outside.

"What do you mean, Edna?"

"He is way over six feet, wears cowboy boots and a Stetson hat, and always a white shirt and string tie, with a single action Colt 45 with ivory grips strapped on his side. What I don't know is what kind of a man he is."

"I can tell you he is a good 'un, and I'm speaking from experience. Hell, Big Jim is a lawman with a heart. Rough as a cob he is, but that ain't all he is. Why, I've heard tell he is a marriage counselor for married folks, and when kids get in trouble for sowing their wild oats, he sends them to church rather than jail. Yet if he puts the word out that he wants to see you, then you know he knows what you have done, and you better get your butt to his office. Did you know he was a Texas Ranger?"

I shook my head.

"Yep, back in the 40's, and since being elected sheriff in 1946, he has been the president of the Texas Sheriff Association and was elected to the Texas Hall of Fame of the Texas Rangers. Yes sir, you won't find a better man on this here earth than James Flournoy."

On November 27, 1961, me and Jessie signed the papers. I agreed to Jessie's askin' price of thirty thousand. With pride, I paid fifteen hundred down in cash with the promise to pay two hundred a month for the house with eleven acres, and all the furniture and fixtures that were conveyed. And thank God, Della would stay on. In fact, she was getting a raise.

And the best part of the deal was that I wouldn't work that night. Instead, I'd be busy preparing a list of house rules. Tomorrow at breakfast I would announce my ownership of Edna's Fashionable Ranch Boarding House. The rules would be posted and any questions answered.

Then, instead of hangin' around during the long afternoon, I'm gonna search for a house to rent. The sooner, the better. Never again will I sleep under the roof of the Chicken Ranch. When business closes at 3 am, I'll lock up and head to my own place. I'll find a small house nearby in the country.

For the first time in my life, I'll have a home. A place with my stamp on it. Furniture of my choosin', pictures on the walls, a porch swing, and maybe a little kitchen stuff. I'll show up for breakfast with the girls, then do paper work in my office. Bein' back home for a short time in the afternoons would be wonderful. Then when I lock the doors at three, I'll come home to my own bed and dreams.

At last, I would become a businesswoman in a man's world. Not one minute too soon.

EDNA'S FASHIONABLE RANCH BOARDING HOUSE

The transition went off without any whoopla whatsoever. Jessie just packed up and left right after closing time. Her good friend in San Antonio came to get her. So at breakfast on November 28, 1961, I naturally took Jessie's place at the head of the table. I sipped my coffee and looked directly at each of the girls as they settled in their chairs. I was sure none of them was surprised that I was now the madam because I had been managin' the place for years due to Miss Jessie's failin' body. And, I 'speck they were all anxious to hear about any changes I might make.

For sure, I wouldn't be another Miss Jessie. They all knew me well enough to know that from now on the Ranch would be a combination of charm school and a Marine boot camp.

I am a cut above. I've always felt that way, for no reason I could figure. And no doubt, these girls see in my green eyes—some have called cold—the total power that is now mine over them and the ranch.

"Ladies, go ahead and help yourself to breakfast. I hope all of you are feelin' tolerable this morning. The coffee is hot and mighty good this fine day."

I smiled and from the large white platter took a giant biscuit before continuin'. "As I'm sure you all know, Jessie Williams has sold me this place and it is goin' on the tax records as Edna's Fashionable Ranch Boarding House. I'll be referrin' to you as my boarders. I'll take seventy-five percent of your earnings, and that is a bargain for you, because you have no expenses. I'll provide the food, rent, laundry, and the weekly visit to the doctor. I can see you each makin' three hundred a week if you stay busy. Now tell me if you can, where or how an uneducated gal can clear that kind of money these days?"

My hot biscuit had never tasted so good. I licked my lips. "I also want you to know it is time you were more comfortable while you work. I'm gonna put window air-conditioners in your rooms."

Cheers went up and everyone clapped. Now was the time to tell them about the other changes.

I waved my hand for quiet and began the prepared speech slowly and with authority. "Our new hours of operation are going to be from 3:00 pm to 3:00 am. I know that's a twelve-hour workday, but you won't be workin' every minute. There will be a dinner break around six on an individual basis, and of course you will have free time between customers. How much you work will be your call, but it goes without sayin' I won't put up with any boarder who is idle more than they work. Besides, you are only here to make money, right? I'd like to think

you each got yourself a plan. In my book, whorin' is only a means to an end. Any questions or comments?"

I didn't think of myself as a dictator. But quiet reigned as the boarders ate their breakfasts and waited for what was next.

"If you have a boyfriend or husband, you will tell them to show up at 3:15am and they wait outside, 'cause I ain't havin' no one in this house who ain't conductin' business. I'm gonna have to get after those Aggies who come here just to dance with you pretty girls. I'm thinkin' if I make Thursday night a special, that will keep me from havin' to shoo them out of here in a friendly way."

I shook my head and waved my hand for emphasis as I cleared my throat. "I know Miss Jessie didn't allow for this, but times are different these days. The girls in town and about these parts are giving it away, so we are gonna have to sell something other than the missionary position. What I'm sayin' is, if the man wants any sexual frills you are okay with, then that's fine with me. But do remember, you ain't his slave and if it is something rough or distasteful to you, by God, he ain't havin' it in my house. Never forget, you are in charge, not him. Your bedroom door is never locked and it is my job to see to it you are safe. Just keep a bureau drawer left slightly open to show an interestin' assortment of erotic para-phernalia that might tempt even the two-stroke man to go for the forty-dollar package. After all, this is about money. And another thing, use an antiseptic douche after each job, but I think you do that already."

I smiled then and looked at each of the girls. They reminded me of myself some ten years back. I'll make life as good as I can for them, but it has to be a two-way street. "I'm gonna post this, but I want you all to listen to me now real careful."

The rules and regulations were hot off last night's press. I changed my voice to fit the occasion. "I, Edna Arretha Milton, a femme sole trader, own this building and all the furnishings, also 11.32 acres of land duly recorded in the Fayette County Courthouse, La Grange, Texas 78945.

"This place nor I have any connections whatsoever with any other place, mob, or syndicate of any type. This place is individually owned by me. To whom it may concern to all livin' on these premises:

"If anyone here is an illiterate or of subnormal intelligence, they had better have someone read and explain this to them. Read this regularly (about once a month) if you want to live here. These rules will be followed by all boarders, no exceptions. Anyone havin' no intentions of followin' these rules might just as well leave now."

It made me feel good to see the faces around the breakfast table look down at their plates and then to each other before givin' me their attention again. Clearly they felt controlled and that is what I aimed for. My way or the highway.

"Absolutely no narcotics are permitted on these premises. If any narcotics are found or suspected, the law will be called immediately.

"Drinking is not permitted during visitin' hours and anyone doing so will be asked or ordered to leave.

"In short, dope heads, pill heads, and drunks are not permitted to live here regardless of who they are.

"Thieves, liars and robbers are not needed or wanted here. When I ask a boarder a question, I demand an honest to-the-point answer.

"What you do away from here and away from this county is your business as long as it has no reflection on me or my business."

I glanced around the table at my boarders. I had everyone's attention so I concluded by standin' up and sayin' one last thing: "This ain't no rule, but I want every last one of you to be clear about this. You havin' a pimp or husband, givin' some man your money is purely stupid. You don't need him. He ain't gettin' you any business and I'm keepin' you safe. Think about it and if you need help gettin' rid of him, I'll be happy to do it. And another thing, there won't be no more college co-eds workin' here in the summer. If you want to tell your john you are in college over in Austin, that don't hurt nothin'. In fact, it can help your idea of yourself and that's always a good thing."

I pushed my chair in and smiled again at everyone. "My office door is always open to you, and remember I'm the one who needs to know if you got a problem. And it's a good idea if you don't gather in each other's rooms. Use the private area to visit or read. Beds are not to be wallowed in with your chums. That's what hogs do. And it goes without sayin' much about it, but I ain't havin' no hanky-panky goin' on between any of my boarders. Is that understood?"

I could feel their heads nod and their eyes on me as I left the table. I walked slowly to my office and closed the door. I sat down in Jessie's chair. Heart pumpin', I felt on top of the world. At last, I was a businesswoman and one who had just bought a thrivin' one. Since the fifties, students, farmers, servicemen, politicians, and salesmen had put the Chicken Ranch on the national map. My house now operated at maximum capacity of sixteen girls and business was good, especially on weekends.

I had seen the line of customers waitin' in front of the cement stoop wind halfway round the big white house. And thank God, Della was stayin' on. She even doubled as a maid and sometimes the cook. Della knew the clients well and she knew when to unlock the screened door and when to turn a customer away. And although she was black, she didn't admit visitors who were black or Mexican. Beginnin' today, she would simply say, "Sorry honey, I can't let y'all come in. Them's Miss Edna's rules."

I opened the new ledger and noted my plan to put AC in every bedroom. Sure the rooms were comfortable, but the furnishings were drab, but I wasn't gonna change the cheap, imitation Early American nightstands, beds, and dressers. The washable chenille bedspreads in magenta, red, gold, and turquoise would have to last a while longer, too. Thank goodness the six bathrooms were plenty, and the bedrooms were all equipped with their own tiny lavatory cubicle for cleaning the customers before the date and the boarder afterwards. When I can afford it, I'll do something about that awful living room. Maybe walnut paneling, flowered drapes with pink and green sequins, and floral carpeting would spiff it up.

Yes sir, I had bought a right good business and it

was gonna stay that way. One day I'll buy my own house in town and a fancier car than I have now. Drivin' to Bastrop to bank once a month is gonna make me feel right prosperous. Hell, I'll be making big deposits and everyone in the bank will know what a capable businesswoman I am. Finally, finally I have myself a life.

I looked forward to Sheriff Jim's visit. He came by every evening to check on things. Of course we knew each other, but I had never sat down to talk to him as the owner. He had never said more than a 'how ya do', but now that would change. His protection was major and so I would get to know this man.

I poured him a cup of coffee in my office and after he offered his congratulations, I opened up the conversation by asking about his life. Inwardly, I grinned. No man alive can resist talkin' about himself.

"I know you been here in La Grange since the 40's but I don't know nothin' 'bout what you done before."

Jim smiled. "Why hell, Ellie, reins in one hand and a Colt 45 in the other, I spurred a sweat-soaked stallion through the prairies of south and west Texas in pursuit of cattle thieves."

Had he said Ellie? I was caught off guard and I was sure it showed. I felt my face turn red so I lowered my eyes to shuffle papers on my desk while I got myself together before I said, "You called me Ellie?"

"Why not? I'm sure as hell not gonna call you Miss Edna. No disrespect intended, but you gonna be Ellie to me."

I decided not to address this announcement. So instead I said, "And what's sheriffin' like these days?"

"Oh, Lord. Nowadays I drive my Ford LTD to the courthouse to battle the University of Texas lawyers hired to spring their clients on technicalities. In many ways, I liked patrolling the 44-county area across West Texas from Del Rio to El Paso better."

I was quick on the draw. "Tell me about those times, Jim." If he was gonna call me Ellie, I would drop 'sheriff.'

I had made the right move and he didn't react to me callin' him Jim. I could tell he loved the memories and was up for sharin' them. So I put an expectant look on my face and gave him my undivided attention.

"I'd pull my horse trailer into Big Bend as far as I could, then horseback it the rest of the way. I was watching for smugglers. There were these big mercury mines where they dug mercury out of the ground to use in the war effort. Mexicans would come across and steal it by putting saddlebags on mules to get it back across the river. Then they would turn right around and bring it back across the border again to sell it to the federal government. As a Ranger, I'd ride along the Rio Grande looking for hidden trails and wait until the smugglers came along so I could rush in and arrest them. Actually, the whole thing got pretty tedious."

"Well, like everyone else in Fayette County, I'm glad you are our sheriff. I know I can count on you like Jessie did. And, I want to tell you up front that you will have my complete cooperation."

I liked the man. He knew his job and he wasn't uppity. There wasn't nothin' in his manner that suggested he expected any privileges with me. Sure, I am much younger than Jessie, but our relationship will be the same. Friendly, but strictly business. House rules were for me, too.

Besides, the last thing I needed or wanted was any personal involvement with a man. Maybe in another decade, but I wasn't holdin' my breath. I had had enough sex to last me a lifetime. If I ever let a man into my life, it won't be about sex. And rememberin' Ben was gonna be easier from now on. Another perk for this new businesswoman.

As the tall sheriff got up to leave, I shook his hand and mentioned that I'd be looking for a place near the Ranch to rent.

"Why, Ellie, if you ain't something. I've never heard tell of a madam not living at her brothel." He smiled as he walked out, shaking his head. "Yes sir, if you don't beat all."

Della had spotted her asleep on the stoop. A real young one she was, and in a bad way. Mighty dirty, sunburned, matted blond hair, and bloody feet showin' through her worn out shoes. Della told me later she hated to touch her, but she hadn't moved an inch with her just callin' to her.

"Now, miss. Come on and wake up. Breakfast is cooking and I 'speck you be mighty hungry."

Della was in charge since it would be a few minutes before I got there. This sad gal would have to shower before she could go to the table, but she didn't have no suitcase with her. Mercy! What a little tramp.

Finally Amy woke up and let Della help her up and guide her to the bathroom. It was the shower that really woke her up. How many days had it been? Walkin' and hitchin' rides all the way from Rusk, in east Texas, had taken its toll. Never had she been so dirty or so hungry, but she had made it. By God, she had made it to the Chicken Ranch.

Della opened the bathroom door and shoved a clean dress at her. She could smell breakfast so she didn't wait to be invited.

Amy made it to the table and it seemed like she could feel the eyes of everyone on her as she sat down slowly without looking around.

"And just who might you be?" I said. The girl was a beauty, but clearly done in. A starvin' tramp didn't come to the door every day.

Amy looked to the head of the table to see my cold eyes in a smilin' face. "My name is Amy Peterson and I have been making my way here from Rusk, Texas. I got a couple of rides, but I've mostly been walking."

A motherly voice out of my hard mouth said, "Okay, Amy. Eat you all the breakfast you want and then I'll see you in my office."

The breakfast guest reached for the biscuit platter. Food! Oh, bless Jesus, there was food all over the huge table. No one said another word to her so she ate and ate and ate.

After breakfast, Amy came into my office and sat down without makin' a sound. I hadn't finished writin' in my ledger yet so Amy had time to look around the small room. There was only the large desk in the middle of the room and one comfortable chair to sit in. No family photos anywhere, but there was one pretty painting of red roses. The frame was a narrow gold one and the vase in the picture held roses of deep, deep red. The roses were hypnotizin'.

"Tell me about yourself, Amy. What was so awful that you were willin' to walk most of the way from East Texas?"

Then I watched her sit up straighter and put her shoulders back. She looked me right in the eyes without any sign of embarrassment. Clearly she wasn't a tramp. At first her words were tentative, but they grew forceful as she told her story.

"After my ma died a couple of years back, there weren't no good reason to stay put. I was the only girl in the house and both my old pap and my three brothers did me any time they took a notion, which was near about every night fer one of 'em. I finished high school, but that's all I done with my sorry life. I'm eighteen and I don't know nothin' cept workin' and screwin'. I kept the house and did the cookin' and washin' for those four bastards, who I don't plan on ever seein' again in this lifetime."

I smiled at her and said, "If you graduated from high school, you have done something. Education is a mighty valuable thing. But what brought you to the Chicken Ranch?"

"I overheard some men talkin' at the City Café. I wasn't no waitress, but I did bus tables for a couple of months. Anyway, they was sayin' what a nice place this was and how pretty the girls were. So I got to thinkin' that if I could just get here you might hire me on. But first you'd need to teach me how to be pleasant to the men folks. I know what they do, but I don't know how to act about it so as to get paid. And too, I don't have no money or clothes, but if you could give me a little advance, I'd pay you back right off. Miss Edna, there ain't one soul in Texas who cares a whoop about me. No ma'am, I'm as good as an orphan."

My usual good humor vanished and misery took its place. Flashes of Uncle Ken and Red on top of me and my brother treatin' me like I was no count, took me over. So Amy's story wasn't all that unusual. All of the boarders have had their backs up against the wall at some time in their lives. There are many reasons why prostitution is the oldest profession in the world.

It took me a minute before I could say, "Okay, Amy, as it happens I do have a bedroom vacant as of last Tuesday. And since you've been on the receivin' end of a man, you know what it's about. However, unlike with yo' dad and brothers, these men are payin' for you. They have chosen you, so it is your job to make sure they enjoy themselves. Make a point to call them by name; keep a smile on your pretty face; say complimentary things to them; and act like you think they are the best thing since sliced bread when it comes to screwin'. Your job is as much about how you act as it is the sex. No one will ever hurt you. You are safe here and always remember you are actually in charge, he just mustn't know it. And before I forget it, my house rules are written and easy enough to understand. I'll take you into town in a little while for a suitable evening dress and a few around-the-house clothes. You won't need much."

Amy smiled for the first time and declared she would be a good boarder and work hard. She started to get up, but I motioned for her to stay.

"Now, I want to know what your plans are. Bein' a whore is only good for gettin' you to what you can do with your life. I encourage my boarders to have a plan."

"I'm so glad you asked 'cause I've been dreamin' of having a beauty shop. I used to fix all my girlfriends' hair and I'd give anything to have my own business. Maybe in Austin or Houston. But I guess I could get by just bein' an operator."

"Absolutely not! There ain't no reason in this world why you can't own your shop and have a fine business. Why, just a few years back one of the girls here, Maizie, saved up her money and got to Austin where she got trainin' to be a nurse. It took her a while, but she made it. Lived at the YWCA and worked in the kitchen for school money. Now she is a nurse at one of the big hospitals there and lives in her own apartment with a roommate. I hear from her every Christmas."

"Miss Edna, that's mighty encouragin'. I'll make up my mind to go to beauty school and take it from there. And no one will have to know I worked here at the Chicken Ranch. Meaning no offense. You takin' me in like this is the Lord's blessing."

After Amy left, I was alone with my thoughts. I was livin' my plan. My place was famous all over the country. I make lots of money and I call the shots for everyone under my roof, not countin' Della. So why was it that I still wasn't even close to being happy? Maybe Jessie had been right sayin' happiness was for four year olds.

I had my own rent house, but no one ever came to visit. The merchants spoke to me in town, but I never got any kind of an invitation to anything. The only adults I ever talked to, who weren't customers or boarders, were Della and Jim.

It surprised me some that bein' a successful business-woman wasn't a full life. I sit in the porch swing with my first cup of coffee and lay in my bed at night with nothing to think about but business. I don't want for nothin', but even so, I'm empty and solitary. The year after year sameness is rottin' my soul. Not countin', of course, the rare times I have to fire my 38-caliber Smith and Wesson into the ceiling to impress an unruly customer. I'm beginning to wonder if I'm needing yet another plan?

"Good grief, what nonsense," I said aloud to the empty room. "Time to take Amy to town for some clothes at the New York Store. Think I'll take her by the Blue Bonnet Beauty Salon for a haircut, too. Amy will enjoy seein' what the Hattermans have done to the place. She needs the inspiration. Sittin' here diggin' up bones is foolishness."

Later in the day I realized it had been a fine day shoppin' for Amy. I love seein' the need in the eyes of my girls. With any luck at all, that one will work hard and get her pretty self out of here before too long. As I poured myself another glass of tea I noticed the time. About then I heard his patrol car pull up.

"Jim, you're a little late this evening. Did you have a bad day?"

"Oh hell, Ellie. Today was one of those days when I was tempted to just ride off into the sunset. Unhappy prisoners in the jail always gets me down."

I laughed and offered him some iced tea. What would I do without these nightly visits with Jim? I'd give him a minute to unwind before gettin' to one of his many stories.

"I'll be right back. I need to check with Della about something. Drink your tea and calm down. Tonight I want to hear about how you met your wife." I patted his shoulder as I walked past the chair. Jim was the only man friend I had ever had.

Sure enough Jim was in a better mood when I got back to the office. "Well, let me see. I do believe the very first time I ever laid eyes on her was in 1928. She was sweeping a porch at the country store and I couldn't take my eyes off her. I guess it was love at first sight."

"It can happen that way, I know. I loved a young man once and it happened sudden like. Yeah, I sure enough know what you mean."

He didn't show any interest in my story and I wasn't surprised. Men weren't much interested in a woman's story. Except for Ben, of course.

Jim smiled with the memory of it. "A few months later, there was a box supper at the West Point School House and I was hell bent to leather to buy her box, and I did, too. I outbid every last one of those other boys. We married the next year and been at it ever since. No kids though. That's been hard on her, but she don't say much about it anymore."

The mood always changed at the breakfast table when one of the boarders had been let go. But today even Della wasn't talkin'.

I knew I'd need to speak to her later, but for now I turned my attention to the silent table. "Rules are rules and they are for everyone. This ain't no secret, so why the long faces?"

Not one of the silent girls even looked at me, so I continued. "Sure, Marion was a good worker and she had been here for over five years, but that don't make her special. And for that matter, none of you are either. Not if bein' special means you can break the rules."

One might think I didn't enjoy these sessions, but you'd be wrong. I knew best and it would always be my way or the highway.

"I do everything I can to keep you all safe while you earn a shit load of money here and you only have to follow the rules. So let me say one more time what you already know. No involvement with local men, and it's not just for the good of my business. Do you really think a local family is gonna welcome you when junior brings you home? You want to be considered the worst sinner to ever join the church? Think about it."

I buttered my biscuit so as to give them all time for it to sink in. I looked around the table at unhappy faces. How in the world can these women be so stupid? So I took a swig of coffee before goin' on with it.

"It is purely stupid to make a man your ticket out of

here and it don't matter much if he is from La Grange or an Aggie or some salesman from Houston. Why in the hell would you want to turn your life over to someone else anyway? Besides, what if he is just fine, but he up and dies on you. What you gonna do with a bunch of kids to feed and no way to do it? You'd have to go back to whorin' if you weren't too old."

I could never be certain if they understood or not, but one thing was for damn sure, I didn't mince no words. I really did care for all of them, but it sure tested my metal to put up with their blindness to how the world is.

Now, talkin' to Della was another matter. That black woman was an institution at the Ranch and I respected that. So after breakfast I carefully asked her to come to my office when she had time. I sure didn't order her to, but she came.

"I want to know what's on your mind. I can tell you are frettin' about me lettin' Marion go."

Della stood in the open office door, and she took her time movin' over to the one big chair to sit down. "I guess it is just gettin' harder and harder for me to see how you ain't changin' with time. I keep thinkin' you'll come around, but you ain't. That's all."

I was put off, to say the least, but I kept the irritation I was feelin' out of my voice. "You'll need to be more specific than that, Della. I've been runnin' this place real good now for seven years, so if I need to change myself, you'll have to tell me how and why."

"Oh, Miss Edna. Sure 'nuf you do a fine job of runnin' the Ranch. Everybody knows that. I'm not talkin' about the Ranch. I'm talking about you. It beats all I've ever seen how you control the girls. I know you does it out of concern for them and yo' business, but it's still control. I keep thinkin' you gonna notice someday that we ain't in control. None of us, black or white."

"Are you suggestin' my rule about not gettin' involved with local men is too controllin' over their lives?"

"No, ma'am, I ain't. I'm sayin' when one of them takes a shine to some man, you don't just knee-jerk them out of here. Your gals respect you and I'm thinkin' they would listen to you. Hear their story and then use your experience to point up the likelies, the good along with the bad. I know your story and that is why I'm suggestin' this. You have had the worst and the best of it, so you understand how it can go. Let them talk. Listen to their story and that will help them make up their own minds. I'm thinkin' we all have our own best answers."

I had to laugh. "Why, Della, I didn't know you were a philosopher."

"Now, Miss Edna. Don't you go makin' fun of me. I don't even know what that word means. But I'm gonna say one last thing, then I'm done. You wantin' all these gals to wear your suit. That's the control I'm talkin' 'bout. Just 'cause you won't have no man in your life don't mean that is the best way for all of them. I've done noticed things go the way they does for a reason, and most times it can't be figured. Plan or no plan."

I went home for my afternoon rest, but I couldn't get Della's words off my mind. Am I trying to control them or protect them? Finally I decided that if it was control, it was for their own good. Now, how bad could that be? Maybe I'll talk to Jim about it this evenin' when he comes by.

Jim came in the back door waving a magazine. "Ellie, bet you haven't read this article in the Texas Observer. Here it is on page 8 called 'The Chicken Ranch'. Some guy named Saul Friedman wrote it. Ever heard of him?"

"No, I ain't, but that don't surprise me none. Reporters don't have to know much about my business to write about it. Have you read it?"

"Hell, yes, I've read it. Ain't half bad, but you're right. He didn't get it all straight, but that don't matter. It's a right good article. I'll leave it for you to read. How does it feel to own such a famous place as the Chicken Ranch?"

I thought a minute before smilin'. "It feels good enough. I work at it, you know. Don't come accidental. Every goddamn day, as Jessie once said."

Changin' the subject to what I wanted to hear about was done without Jim takin' notice. "You kill any desperados today?" I lit another cigarette and got comfortable for Jim's story.

"Not today, but I can tell you about a bank robbery in Carmine many years back. Yes sir, me and my deputy got word in time to get there while it was going on. This one guy was keeping watch outside the bank with his 45 automatic. I pulled out my gun and got him covered good before I snuck up real quiet like and just lifted that pistol right out of his hand. After handcuffing the look-out and shoving him out of the way, me and my deputy smashed in the side door of the bank. The robber spun around and aimed his pistol at the deputy, but as he did, one of the tellers pulled his own weapon out from behind the counter, and shot the bandit through the back of the head. When we lifted his body off the floor, he was still holding onto the bag full of money and his gun."

"Jim, by God, you got a story for anything I can think up to ask ya'. What I'm wonderin' is if you're truthful?"

I laughed and it felt good. I glanced at the magazine article and noticed it was almost two pages long. Maybe I'd start it later that night when I had time to read.

June 21, 1968. *The Texas Observer*. By Saul Friedman on page 8, The Chicken Ranch.

Going north, State Highway 71 begins at Palacios, on the coast, pauses at Blessing, then takes off for the hills where it's famous. It's called the 'Texas Hill Country Trail' north and west of Austin and it gets attention from land speculators, tourists, reporters, and the state highway department as it travels through the heart of Lyndon Land.

To the south, between Austin and Columbus, 71 is being replaced by a super highway and to assuage the fears of folks along the old road, it has been designated part of the stuff of history. Blue and white signs with an upraised arm and rifle, calling the highway the 'Texas Independence Trail,' mark the route. This ought to amuse at least two generations of Texas menfolk. For them, Highway 71 has been part of the history of stuff; their favorite spot on the road has been an obscure turnoff, just south of La Grange. About a quarter-mile east of the main road, at the end of a dirt and gravel lane, in the middle of a cow pasture surrounded by pin oaks and willows, is the Chicken Ranch – the oldest established continuously operating non-floating whorehouse in Texas – maybe the nation.

It would not be good to be more specific about its location. The law knows where it is, but believes there is no sense killing a good thing. Besides, any freshman at Texas A&M, the University of Texas, or the Texas legislature who gets money from home, or elsewhere, can find out where it's at.

The dirt road, which is posted ("Bad Curves" and "Watch for Loose Livestock") and looked after by helpful Fayette county officials, leads only to the Chicken Ranch. And when one drives up for the first time, there is no mistaking what it is. In the sultry heat of a Texas summer night, shiny cars surround the house and wait in the darkness. The only sound is the loud whisper of a dozen air conditioners in the louvered windows of a dozen rooms.

The house, a one-story, white, clapboard building, is rambling and jerry-built because a room at a time has been added over the years as business increased. There was, incidentally, no interruption in the commerce within during construction; indeed, the carpenters often enjoyed long afternoon breaks, which diminished their hourly wages.

A gravel area surrounds the house for the sporty, late-model cars of the girls around back, and in the front the pickup trucks and rented cars of the day customers, and the collegiate Volkswagens and executive Pontiacs of the night trade. Over the screened front door is a yellow light, to keep bugs away. Arrayed around the house are spotlights to discourage burglars, peeping toms, and assorted other troublemakers. During the busy nighttime hours on Fridays and Saturdays a local, off-duty law officer is hired to patrol the area against drunks or unruly students, for the Chicken Ranch is anxious to protect its long reputation for being peaceful and law-abiding – prostitution aside, naturally.

There is a reason its customers, law officers, politicians, and even the folks in Fayette County protect the Chicken Ranch. It's a throwback, the last of the oldtime houses of pleasure which used to spice the life of Texas. In Houston there was a place where the madam kept the girls honest by counting towels. In Bell County there was a house in the country which the district attorney and most of his cronies visited until one day when he appeared sheepishly and reluctantly at the front door, having been forced by some churchwomen to lead a raid. "Not now, George." The owner of the establishment hollered from inside. "The law has got me surrounded." And of course, Hattie Valdez' place in Austin was one of the busiest spots in town during a session of the legislature. It was destroyed by fire a few years ago and all that was left standing was the chimney.

There are still places in Galveston and Sealy and other parts of the state, but they get closed now and again as reform movements and new police officers come and go. In the big cities there are few, if any houses now. Hookers, some of them dope addicts, most of them working for pimps, hustle on the streets or in hotels. More respectable looking girls work as stenographers or behind counters during the day and answer calls at night. But the girls on the streets and the call girls prices are too steep for the student, the farmer, or the drummer without an expense account.

The Chicken Ranch has always been priced just right for the more plebeian trade, and with its seclusion, its homelike comforts, its carefully screened girls, and its reputation for staying out of trouble, it has remained in business for nearly 55 years. The Ranch was opened by two sisters who had made a modest bundle among the roughnecks and wildcatters around Beaumont after the turn of the century when the Spindletop oil boom began, then decided to settle down and let the business come to them. They picked their spot south of LaGrange, in the hills above the Colorado River, because it was secluded, yet not far from the colleges and large cities, and on the way to the state capital, where every business and political hustler had to come. After a few years one of the sisters left to get married and the other, whom we shall call Miss Sarah, owned it until a few years ago when she died in her eighties.

Before prohibition Miss Sarah's place was a rough and Texan version of the more classic houses of the evening in New Orleans. There were drinks and dancing to the latest music in the big front parlor of the house, and there was no pressure on the girls or the customers to get their business done and the money paid. Prohibition in Texas took some of the romance and fantasy from Miss Sara's and made it more mercenary. She used to remember how she laughed when the Fayette county sheriff came to her one day. "Miss Sarah. I don't like it any more than you do. But the drinkin' has just got to stop."

It was a measure of the crazy contradictions Miss Sarah encountered in the area around La Grange. It was a strange place to open a whorehouse. Most of the farmers, ranchers, and merchants thereabouts come from German or Slavic stock – religious, prudish, conservative, strict. And yet they've never seriously bothered the Chicken Ranch or the girls who come in to town to do a little shopping. The women must know their menfolk visit the house and even take their sons there the first time to teach them. And the townspeople must know that many travelers hear of La Grange and come through it only because of the Chicken Ranch.

Maybe it's allowed to exist because of the little commerce it brings the town. Or because it's a way to keep 'em down on the farm. Or because the American puritan is unconcerned with sin which falls in some distant forest and cannot be heard.

Once a new woman in town heard about the Ranch and decided she would see it closed. She went to the sheriff who told her it was the first he'd heard of it and he would sure check on it and if it was true, what she heard, he would do something about it. She went to her minister, who smiled benignly and told her indulgently that there were things in this world which simply couldn't be helped. She persisted, nevertheless, and urged her husband, who sold bagged peanuts, popcorn and potato chips and such to groceries and taverns, to join her. One Sunday morning, as they stepped from their house on the way to church, they found the front lawn littered with bags of peanuts, popcorn and potato chips from merchants who wanted the couple to mind their own business or lose it. The one-woman reform movement ended.

During the thirties the depression hit Miss Sarah's, but she stayed open. Her girls gave credit to good customers or accepted payment in farm produce, when they had to. There were so many chickens the girls couldn't eat them all, so they raised them, and the place became known as the Chicken Ranch.

It became so well-known that men from miles around could call the La Grange operator and ask her to tell Miss Sarah to expect a party of two or four or more at ten. During legislative sessions the lobbyists brought the politicians down for an evening. And each year, after the traditional Thanksgiving Day game between the University of Texas and Texas A&M, alumni of the winning school would treat the whole team to a night at the Chicken Ranch – after turkey dinner, of course. That's not done anymore; no need to leave the campus; no need to pay.

The Chicken ranch nearly closed for the first time in about 1962 when then-Attorney General Will Wilson was bucking for governor and crusading against sin in places like Galveston. Miss Sarah became very ill and left her garish, turn-of-the-century bedroom for a hospital in Austin. She wanted to close the place but Hilda, the most veteran employee, volunteered to stay so no customer would be turned away. She and two other girls worked the Chicken Ranch until the heat was off. And when Miss Sarah died peacefully (the newspaper obituaries said she was 'a La Grange businesswoman'), Hilda bought it from the old lady's estate.

As in any business, new blood will tell. Miss Hilda, who is now in her early forties, had the place redecorated (without missing a night's business), hired a dozen new girls, installed a uniformed Negro maid to answer the door and ordered the help to wear fetching sports clothes for the day trade and fashionable cocktail dresses in the evening.

The prices ($10 - $15 for a straight date) did not go up, but girls were now permitted, if they wished, to engage in more exotic and expensive exercises with their customers. The late Miss Sarah had been old-fashioned and would fire a girl she caught catering to the tastes of a 'preevert'. One thing has not changed under the proprietorship of Miss Hilda. Bottles of Coca-Cola are still used for accounting. Each customer is encouraged to buy Cokes, at 50 cents each, for himself and his girl. The extra dollars go for miscellaneous things the girls need; the bottles are counted by the management to keep track of how much business each girl does.

The girls keep about half of what they make and the rest goes to the house, which pays the room and board. The girls live where they work and leave for those few days each month when Mother Nature provides them with time to visit friends and family.

Many of the Chicken Ranch girls have fled to Miss Hilda's from the streets or from knocking around in hotel rooms taking chances on the police or dates with strange hang-ups. The Chicken Ranch is a sanctuary for them. There they find safety and peace and quiet. If they are wild, Miss Hilda turns them back to the streets and their procurers. But that's rarely necessary, for the girls of the Chicken Ranch take some pride in its reputation as a house of good, well-mannered women.

There was a judge, a couple of years ago, who had to decide a child custody case. The ex-husband was suing to take the child from his former wife on the grounds she was a prostitute. When the judge heard that the woman worked at the Chicken Ranch he denied the husband's petition. The woman must be decent if she worked at the Chicken Ranch, he decided. And he secretly remembered the days as a young legislator.

I closed up the magazine, lit another cigarette, and was glad the last of tonight's customers were on their way out. I was in one of my moods. They came around more regular lately, and the mystery of them kept me on edge. I couldn't point to nothing in my life as much of a problem. Every year was pretty much like the last. My bank account was growin', my business was famous; nevertheless, there they came. Those feelings of emptiness and deadness.

The article hadn't screwed up many facts, but somehow the overall truth of it had left me mad at everybody and nobody. On the one hand, it noted the things about the Ranch that had earned it a national reputation as outstandin', yet it is a whorehouse, and as such, subject to public ridicule. And shouldn't that be expected?

After all, why should I have the respect of the world for ownin' a whorehouse, even if it is a famous one? My plan was to be a businesswoman. Am I just now, after all this time, realizin' that ownin' a brothel might not be high on the respectable list? Now, ain't that a kick in the pants. Did I actually think that my plan to be a businesswoman was all that mattered? Bein' a whore was a means to an end, but ownin' the brothel was somehow different. Better. Respectable? Shit, I may be some stupid after all.

I locked up and turned off the lights to the front of the house. As I started the car to take the short drive to my empty house, I remembered Jessie's words, "Just another goddamn day." Maybe I'll bring it up to Jim tomorrow evening.

———

"I don't know what to make of it, Jim." I needed to talk about something besides him and his sheriff stories.

Jim scratched his head. "You mean there's someone who wants to interview you about the Chicken Ranch and they ain't a reporter?"

"Yeah, a Robbie Davis-Floyd who will publish the article in the *Journal of American Folklore*. It's an education-type something. Let me read you what she said it was about: The interest is in my strategic and tactical use of folklore in social interaction."

"Hell, Ellie, I don't know what that means, do you?"

"Not really, but the title is gonna be, *Landlady at La Grange: The Folklore of a Texas Madam*. Now, ain't that somethin'?"

The sheriff just laughed, "I reckon it is, but I don't want you gettin' too big for your britches now."

"Oh, damn it, Jim, you know me better'n that. I'll jest answer the questions I want to and let it go at that. Don't really have all that much time to sit around while some writer takes notes, but honestly, I could use a little change of pace. There are days when I get mighty tired of the same ole same ole."

Jim and I just sat in silence for a while, like we often did. I didn't have no notion what he was thinkin' about, but I was wonderin' where did time go anyway? It is 1971 and that means it has been ten years since buyin' the Ranch off Jessie. Ten years of being a businesswoman, and one who is known well enough to have folks wantin' to interview me. But I ain't foolin' myself none. It ain't so much me as it is the fascination with prostitution. For sure, the good folks want to know what goes on here. I'd laugh if it didn't make me want to scream.

Robbie Davis-Floyd interviewed me at the Chicken Ranch on three separate occasions for approximately four hours each time. Another graduate student, Rita O'Brien, came along to concentrate her study on the 'girls.' I allowed Robbie and Rita to sit down with the girls and even one customer. There had been joke tellin' and just usual conversation, but the published piece weren't hardly nothin' like the interviewin'.

When I read it in the *Journal of American Folklore*, I was shocked and yet seein' the truth in it at the same time. How had the Edna in the article escaped my notice? It didn't make no sense for the truth to be so surprisin' to me. Does Della know me better than I know myself, after all? Good lord. So I read it again and slow, this time.

The face that she constantly presents and maintains is that of a woman who, in general, is mentally stronger than men. I cannot emphasize too much the importance of words in her life. Both she and the girls told us that the prostitute's art is much more mental and verbal than sexual. Men are physically stronger; therefore, to maintain constant control, a prostitute must use words effectively. The girls respect her tremendously because, as one of them said, "She could walk out on this floor right now, take any man to the bedroom, and talk him out of even the deed to his house. She really knows how to handle men." She controls her environment through verbal manipulation.

From the first interview I conducted with her, I realized that she is in complete command of her environment. All the girls obey her rules and regard her wishes, partly from real respect for her wisdom-of-experience, and partly from fear. When I asked her what she did when a girl disobeyed the rules, she answered, "I crown'em, but I hardly ever have to." The rules comprise a code of conduct all the girls must follow – for example, always be nice to the customers whether or not they are nice to you, don't bad mouth the customers to outsiders, don't talk about the workings of the money system at the Ranch, get a health card from the local clinic each week, be on time for meals, and so on. The rules are the verbal framework with which the madam controls her world. I hope to show that her folklore is a key tool in this control, providing her with many opportunities to express herself as unopposed leader of her subculture, while constantly reinforcing and validating that leadership.

In nearly all the jokes told by the madam, the male is the butt. The male is made to appear ridiculous and is outsmarted by a woman, usually a whore. For example, she told us this one: "This guy has his head down between this girl's legs, and he says, "Honey, you've got the roughest pussy." She says, "Well why don't you move up a few inches? You've been lickin' the carpet."

While talking with Rita and me, her voice was sweet and she was pleasantly polite. With Buddy, a customer, she is hard, foul-mouthed, opinionated, and domineering, becoming progressively more so as the interaction continues.

I do not mean to imply by her put-down of Buddy that she puts down all men. Contrary to popular belief, the madam and girls at the Chicken Ranch do not hate men. Her attitude toward men seems to be to place them on a continuum. Toward shy boys, men with small penises, and old men she is gentle and very motherly. She refuses to tolerate men (like Buddy) at the opposite end of the scale, when they try to play the dominance game with her. "They sometimes get drunk and want to assert what men they are," she says, "but they can be put down." She likes and has as friends men who accept her for herself and do not try to dominate her. As far as I can tell, she has no neurotic castration complex and no subconscious wish to be a man. When I asked her if she thought men were superior to women, she replied that physically they were, but "I think you're supposed to judge a person from their eyebrows up, not from what's below the belt."

As previously stated, this madam and the girls feel their most important work is mental and verbal – to remain in control of themselves and their interactions with the customers. She must and does remain in control of all the customers and all the girls. She is, in a sense, super-woman, controlling the women who control the men. She is above all a woman: her folklore shows that she does not place men in a superior position, whores in a inferior position, and unconsciously try to impersonate men while downgrading the whores, the men's sexual objects. When I asked her what she thought of sex in general, she replied, "It's as normal as eatin', goin' to the bathroom, and sleepin' – that's part of the natural function of life." Several times during the interviews, she called her dog Trixie over to the group, saying, "Trixie. Show'em what the good girls do to make money." Trixie obligingly rolls over on her back and waves her legs in the air, which never fails to delight her mistress. To me this is another indication of her full acceptance of herself as a woman and as a whore. She is very aware of the power of both the woman and the whore over the male, whom she sees as biologically dependent on both, and sometimes financially dependent, as in her jingle, "Put on your old gray bustle and get out and hustle 'cause the mortgage on the farm is comin' due."

She identifies strongly with other women, but only with those who fit her concept of womanhood. She has great sympathy for what she terms 'the tired housewife, tendin' a hot stove, and carin' for the kids'. One of her strictest rules is that her girls must never take unfair advantage of the fact that they've been 'sittin' on their can all day and have time to be powered and perfumed' and try to take a married man away from his wife. She expresses, in turn, great contempt for 'sexless women', that is, women who refuse to acknowledge their sexuality. In her opinion, they are inferior to men because they deny the sexuality that is their birthright and their key to the mastery of the male world. Far from wanting to be a man, she has strong pride in her womanhood, which enables her to control both men and other women who lack the same strong pride.

Still seeking the reasons for the consensual existence of the Chicken Ranch in the conservative town of La Grange, I interviewed a number of the townspeople in person and by questionnaire. I found that they split along old-timer and newcomer lines. Most of the old-timers were of Bohemian or Slovakian descent, and had an Old World tolerance for prostitution. They felt that men had needs that must be satisfied, that the presence of the out-of-town prostitutes for this purpose protected the local girls from exploitation, and that one should live and let live. They appreciated the facts that the girls kept to themselves, frequenting only a few places in town (essential stores and the hair salons), and that the madam made substantial contributions to local charities. The newcomers (a newcomer was anyone who had lived in the town for less than ten years), in marked contrast, felt that the presence of the Chicken Ranch gave a bad reputation to the entire town and especially to the local girls, who were often the butt of jokes when they attended out-of-town football games and other events. Nevertheless, the newcomers who had tried in the ten years before my 1971 study to raise public alarms about the Chicken Ranch found themselves ostracized by the old timers. A newcomer newspaper editor once went so far as to print an article in the local paper, and awoke the next day to find his lawn littered with trash. He, like the others, ceased his protest.

The very next evening the first thing out of Jim's mouth was, "Well, Ellie, did you read it?"

"Of course, I read it. Don't know what to make of it, though. Can't take no issue with anything Robbie wrote, but at the same time it sets me on edge some."

"Oh hell, Ellie, I know what riles you about it all. The Chicken Ranch is sure enough a business and you insist on thinking of it as just that. Now, the fact that your business is prostitution is what you ignore and you expect everyone else to, too."

I shot back. "What foolishness, Jim. Could a business make hamburgers and not admit to the hamburgers?"

Jim nodded his head. "Hell, Ellie, I think you try."

"Horseshit." I lit another Camel with a vengeance.

So the days and nights passed, one mostly like the last, for two more years. It was 1973, and by all appearances, gonna be like the past ten for me. Smilin' and welcomin' customers; spendin' money for groceries, clothes and property repairs and improvements in La Grange; donatin' big money to civic needs; makin' weekly deposits in the Bastrop bank; drivin' to the rent house after 3am, 7 days a week; visitin' with Jim every evening, and holdin' court at the breakfast table some mornings.

The Chicken Ranch was my entire life. There was nothin' for me outside of it. Never a movie or dance or church service or party or vacation. And Jim was my only friend. All others just had some connection to the business. The Chicken Ranch was who I was, for how many years now? No need to keep count if there weren't no future plan.

Then almost half way through the year, change came drivin' up the road to my house. It all started with a stakeout by ABC Channel 13 in Houston. Marvin Zindler, reporter for Eyewitness News on that TV station, got an anonymous tip that something dirty was going on outside a little town about 60 miles east of Austin. So in July of 1973, Marvin sent correspondent Len Chapman to check out of the report.

Fred Anderson, news photographer, came along with Chapman for the investigation. He stayed in the van while Len went inside. He took pictures with a small scope camera until one of the girls spotted the camera. Len was asked to leave, but was told he could return without the camera. That is when they left and didn't come back until the next day.

It was too early in the day for customers, so I came out of the house when a car drove up. As soon as I recognized them, I asked Len and Richard Appelt, another photographer now with him, to leave. I identified myself as the owner of the house and property, and I did go on and talk to Len out there in the yard.

"What kind of business are you running?"

"I have a boardin' house here." I spoke easily and with a wry smile.

"Is that all it is?"

"That's enough."

Chapman probed further. "You're not operating a house of prostitution?"

"Whether I am or not doesn't come under the headin'

of your business. I am not gonna go for havin' a bunch of pictures taken unless you are definitely tryin' to close me personally."

"I'm not trying to close you. I want to know what you're operating here."

"You know exactly."

"Who's all involved in the money?"

"I am involved in it and with the others who are here makin' it."

"Who all gets money other than that? Any law officials? Government officials?"

"Certainly the federal government, namely the IRS. You know they get their pint of blood for every quart I get." I motioned to the road. "That's all I've got to say now, so I want you fellas to get back on the road and off my property. I'm askin' you friendly-like, but I can call the sheriff if I need to."

They left, but as I turned back to the house I knew this was gonna be bad. And it was. Because of the nightly TV news coverage for at least a week and the national news and talk personalities jumpin' on the bandwagon, this was too big a stir for it to blow over like the few in years past. Yep, this was definitely different, and all I felt about it was tired.

Chapman headed straight for Austin after he left my place. The wide-open operation of the Chicken Ranch was hard for him to believe. So he got right in to talk to Governor Dolph Briscoe. The governor responded to the report by assurin' Chapman he would talk to Attorney General John Hill. Both recognized the obvious, the Chicken Ranch had to be closed down permanently.

The governor called the sheriff. Jim then closed it with a phone call to me.

"I'll be out to see you in a day or two, Ellie. You just get the girls off the place and put up a closed sign."

"I can do that," I said in a weary voice. Actually, I was more worn out than I realized. Maybe being bone tired was what ailed me cause I didn't feel anything else. Just tired.

All the girls were packed up and gone by the next day. None of them was smilin' because now their lives would be much harder back on the streets and they would have to give their money to some pimp. Della, too, was done in by the news. Her bein' one to keep her feelings to herself, it made me sad to see her head hang so low. No doubt she made the highest salary of any other black woman in Fayette County, maybe even all of Texas. She wouldn't be findin' no other Miss Edna to treat her with respect and pay her so well. For sure, her career was over. Probably back now to cleaning white folks houses. For sure, that is gonna be a bitch!

The house was completely empty and silence reined over the vacant rooms. I was sittin' at the dining room table with my usual cup of coffee and cigarette when Jim's patrol car pulled up. It had been two days since his phone call.

"Come on in, the door is open," I hollered from the dining room.

Jim stepped in with his Stetson hat in one hand and hamburgers in the other. "Hope you're hungry. Got us some fries, too." His voice wasn't the same. It was friendly, but sad and hesitant. And had he ever brought me food?

"I can always eat, even when the sky is fallin'."

"Hell, Ellie, it fell two days ago and look outside, the sun still comes up." He sat down at the table and opened the bag of food. "What you been doing with yourself?"

It wasn't just something to say. I could tell as much from his tone as from all the years we'd been friends, he really cared about me.

"I locked up after all the girls left and went home. Been there sleepin' and watchin' TV until this morning. Figured it was about time for your visit so I high-tailed it over here to make us some coffee."

Both of us chewed in silence. Jim kind of picked at his food, but I ate like a field hand. When had I last eaten?

"So, what's the word around the square? Any good folks out to tar and feather me?"

"Now, Ellie, you know better than that. If it wasn't for all the damn TV news coverage, wouldn't nobody in La Grange be upset at all. Tell you what, I'd better never get my hands on that son-of-a-bitch, Marvin Zindler. This whole blow-up is a pile of shit. Ain't nobody proved any connection between the Chicken Ranch and organized crime, and that's a fact. We both know that is plain ole bullshit, nothin' else. But it's all water under the bridge now. No going back, so what you have to do is sell the place. Shouldn't be all that hard."

I sat there like a stone in the silence, simply drinkin' coffee, smokin' my cigarette, and starin' at Jim. He was my only friend. No family or any other person on the face of this earth knew me or cared about my problems.

No, Jim was the only one. I could see Jim was talkin', but what was he sayin'?

"I got something for you, Ellie." His voice sounded foreign as he fumbled to get his large hand into his shirt pocket. "The title company asked me to give this to you. They are returning your earnest money check. The owners of the house in La Grange you were buying have changed their minds."

Jim slid the check over to me, but he didn't make eye contact. Several heavy minutes passed before he said, "I'm sure sorry. By God, I'm real sorry, Ellie."

I pushed my chair back with a vengeance and tried to stand up, but my legs buckled under me. Jim jumped up to help. He held me close for a few seconds before gettin' me back into the chair.

I crossed my arms on the table and laid my head down on them. My sobs thundered in the vacant house, but Jim didn't try to stop my cryin'. After a while, I got past it. Raised my head up and looked at Jim. "I don't ever cry. Not since Ben didn't come back. Not even when his baby died."

"Well, hell, Ellie, then you are way overdue. Nothing beats a good cry. Are you feeling better now? You should be."

I almost smiled. "I'm going to the bathroom to wash my face. Help yourself to more coffee, I'll be right back."

I got up slowly to test my legs. They were weak but sure. The silence in the house made the long walk down the hall seem sinister. Had this house ever been so silent? All life was gone, and the emptiness wasn't friendly. I washed my face before rushin' to get back to Jim. When he leaves, I thought, I will too. This place gives me the creeps.

"You think I can get a good price for this property?" I said as I sat back down. I was ready to talk.

"No doubt about it, Ellie. It'll sell in no time."

I was feelin' like myself again so I lit a Camel and looked him square in the eyes. I needed to talk to Jim about my life, and now was the time for a new plan. Ready or not.

"Jim, what would you do if you was me?"

"Why, Ellie, I'd head out of Texas like a house afire."

"But I've lived in La Grange since 1952. That's twenty-one years. It is the only home I've ever known."

Jim stood his ground. His voice got a notch higher and his eyes didn't blink. "Not much of a home, if you ask me. Hell, Ellie, they returned your earnest money. Don't that tell you loud and clear you aren't welcome in La Grange?"

I was tempted to cry again. "Oh, I know it, Jim. It's just hard to hear."

"Ellie, you do beat all. How can you disregard never getting an invitation to anything? The way you've never gotten a thank-you for any civic donations, and how you don't exist to anyone outside this Chicken Ranch beats the hell out of me. Goddammit, Ellie, this closing down of your business is a whole new beginning for you. Can't you see that? Maybe you should see it as a blessing, I'm thinking."

Later that evening, restin' in my porch swing as the sun went down was a new experience for me. The glass of red wine was a plus, too. I had to do something besides sleep, and thinkin' about what Jim had said earlier today was the thing to do.

Start with the pluses: lots of money in the bank; property that will sell; a good car I know how to drive; no one to say I can't do anything I want, and I'm only forty-five years old.

The minuses are: I have no idea what I want to do; I am not educated to do anything other than whorin' and bein' a madam, and I've never thought about livin' anywhere else.

The sun had set and my wine bottle was empty. As I staggered over to open the screen door and turned on the light in the house, I decided to do what I preached to the girls . . . make a plan.

FINALLY, MEN AS LEARNING EXPERIENCES

Sayin' goodbye to Jim was hard, even though he was quick to remind me that we would be keepin' in touch. After all, he would see about the sale of my property. For sure, it was a comfort to know I could trust him because he would have my best interests at heart.

Sayin' goodbye to La Grange, not so much. After the Come-to-Jesus meetin' with Jim and a few nights on my porch swing with bottles of wine, I got busy plannin' my future. I started with 'where.' Out of Texas was a certainty. How about mountains? Snow in the winter and cool summertime weather would be good. A city with all kinds of people and a variety of things to do. A city with educational opportunity for adults and colleges. If I was gonna reinvent myself, I'd have to get educated. Tucson, Arizona, was one consideration, but the other, Santa Fe, New Mexico, won out.

Every book and article I read in the La Grange Library created more and more excitement for me. With each passin' day, since the forced closin' of the Chicken Ranch, I read more about Santa Fe, and this brought a stir into my soul like none I had ever known. Everything I read added to my growin' sense that I had found my future. Its location on a plateau at the base of the Sangre de Cristo Mountains at an elevation of seven thousand feet meant snowy winters and nice mild summers. Now that would be a site better climate than Texas.

The books I read told about four centuries of Spanish and Mexican rule, and of the Pueblo cultures that have been there for hundreds more. I could just picture myself drivin' around to these ancient places on a Sunday afternoon, learnin' about the past. Might be nice to think about something other than the day I was livin'. The town's central Plaza had been the site of bullfights, gunfights, political rallies, promenades, and public markets since the early 17th century. But nowadays it was the place to go to hear music and dance on weekends. Imagine that! Gettin' to dance, at last. Christmas time would be a glory, too. I'd join all the other people walkin' Canyon Road. A travel book from the library had pictures of this ancient street, on Christmas Eve when it's covered with snow, scented by piñon fires burnin' in luminarias along the road and echoin' with the voices of carolers and happy families. Could it be possible that Santa Fe has something scheduled almost every night of the week all year long? From music concerts and dance performances to theatrical offerings by local and touring groups. Lord amighty, I'd have me a fine life. I'd have things to do all the time and people, who didn't know my past, to do it with.

I kept seein' the title, Santa Fe, The City Different, and that label called to me. I not only could have different physical surroundings, but I could be a different person. I could become educated.

It wasn't too late to have a career. I could be a professional something. I could buy a home. I could have friends and go places with them. I could shed my old skin like a snake, and be someone brand new. I'd be like that Phoenix bird I'd read about, arisin' out of ashes.

By the time I closed my bank account in Bastrop and packed the car for my drive west, I was totally forward thinkin' and even halfway hopeful I might find redemption. Justifyin' my past as the only choice I had at the time was now no longer a good use of my thinkin' time.

I had done the right thing to become the owner of a brothel. It was the only thing I could have done at the time. How else would I have the large amount of money I now have? It was the best plan at that time.

But now, thanks to the hands of fate and that pompous son of a bitch, Marvin Zindler, I have another shot at a new life. A new me. If I stop feelin' belittled and insulted, I'll get on down the road, and that's just what I'm gonna do. I will learn to talk like an educated person, think new thoughts, and meet new people, and maybe even get past my habit of controllin' every thing and every body. If Della knew, she'd be proud of me. By damn, Jessie, it is a new day. Not another goddamn one from now on.

The two-day drive from La Grange to Santa Fe was almost a religious experience, God or no God. I had never felt stronger or well rested. Money in my purse and an excitin' destination made my spirits soar.

The long stretches of highway gave me plenty of time to envision my new life. And the last few miles from Clines Corner to Santa Fe took my breath away. The huge rocks, the mountains in the distant north, the variety of cactus and the fresh air minus Texas heat and humidity.

I decided to exit Interstate 25 at Saint Francis Street. It was mid-afternoon so the traffic was light. I just kept drivin' straight north until Saint Francis got me all the way to downtown. No need to shop around for a place to stay because at first glance the La Fonda Hotel looked historic and invitin'. A nap to rest up from the long drive and then a walkin' tour around the plaza and some Mexican food for dinner. The last thought I had after lyin' down across the beautiful bed was, 'life is good.'

It was hard to remember it was August because the slight breeze was so nice. To stretch my legs and to get a feel for the place I strolled all around the plaza. People still shopped, and the locals sat on the park benches enjoyin' the live music from the bandstand.

I sat down next to the park statue and got carried away by the Mexican music, happy people, and beautiful evening. When anyone smiled at me, I smiled back. No one knew who I was and that was precious to my soul or whatever was left of it. Tomorrow I'll find a real estate agent. My own home in this wonderful city was what I needed first.

The next morning, I couldn't help but notice the grand lady at the table next to me in the hotel dining room. She was busy talkin' to a young couple about some property. Her silver hair reached past her waist, held back on the side by a large Southwestern hairclip. Her full black skirt almost covered her cowboy boots. Silver and turquoise jewelry decorated her ears, and both arms and hands.

But it was her eyes that told me that she was the one. Those sky blue sparklin' eyes in the tanned face told me I could trust her.

When the three of them got up from their breakfast table I cautiously got her attention. "Excuse me, please. I am new to Santa Fe and am lookin' to buy a home here. Am I correct in thinkin' you are a realtor?"

The woman turned her attention away from the couple and nodded with a smile. "My name is Denise DeValle. Let me give you my card. Do call me and together we will find the property you want. I have lived here all my life, so I know it like the back of my hand. I'll be happy to help you."

I thanked her and carefully put the business card she handed me in my purse. Three days later, the hunt was on.

"Edna," Denise said, "this is a Stamm House and they are considered the best built houses in Santa Fe. You will like the location, too, here in the south part of town. It is only one bedroom and bath, but you said you weren't looking for anything large."

I hadn't budged from beside Denise's car since gettin' out. I wanted time to inspect the outside before goin' in. The house was the typical pale red stucco with a patio enclosed by a piñon wood fence. Over the flat roof

I could see the top of a very tall tree in the backyard and there were four cedar trees along the north front curb. On the south side of the yard there was a tall piñon pole fence separatin' this property from the neighbors.

I liked the large picture window across the front of the house. So far, so good. "Let's go in," I said.

In the south corner of the living room stood a fireplace. In fact, it was really one big room with a kitchen on the north end, the dining area in the middle and then the living room. One nice-sized bedroom and bath and tiny utility room, and that was it. I was glad to see the garage. Most of the properties only had carports, if that.

Denise announced, "The address is 111 Calle Anna Jean."

I smiled and said, "I'll take it and I have cash."

I closed on the Calle Anna Jean within two weeks and moved in with what precious little I had escaped Texas with. Then without rushin' at it while I enjoyed the shopping, I devoted almost a month to furnishin' my home. Of course, I went with the southwest motif. Everything, from the set of six dishes to the livin' room furniture, was a combination of Native American and rustic cowboy. I even bought myself a pair of cowboy boots one day while out shoppin' for a washer and dryer. I would need them when I got around to goin' dancin'. Accordin' to what I read in the Friday *New Mexican* newspaper, the Paramount on Sunday nights and Rodeo Nights on Friday and Saturday nights were the two best dance places.

By then it was September, the days were no longer kind of hot and there were so many hikin' trails close in to Santa Fe. I was motivated to exercise, a new thing for me. With the house all together and time to get outside, I read about the selection of hikin' trails. My favorite quickly became the one that skirted Saint John's College. I would walk a ways and then stop and sit on some rock and gaze at the sky or the southwestern vegetation. There were always people on the well-marked trail and it still thrilled me to have them speak and smile. How long will it take, I wondered, to feel worthy of the notice of people? I am in a new world, bein' a new me, but in my head my past still hasn't let go. I don't ever on purpose think about it, but the feelings around my past still try to ruin my day. How long? I wonder how long it will take to be rid of my Texas past.

Some days I'd get in the car to poke around in nearby villages. Madrid was the most fun. The old saloon there had the best buffalo burgers and I laughed every time I read the sign over the door, "There isn't a town drunk in Madrid. We take turns." Once a coal mining town, now artists and craftspeople had arrived.

One Saturday night, I drove over to listen to the live music and dance. True, the people there were mostly couples and a handful of loud twenty-year-olds, but that was okay. One ole cowboy asked me to dance several times and that was enough.

Later that night, openin' the door to my own home and seein' my beautiful new things was the perfect end to yet another wonderful day. I no longer lived goddamn days. Not in New Mexico.

It was late September and time to get started with gettin' an education. Sure I was forty-five, but after one trip to the downtown library, I found out about the New Mexico Adult Education Association. As an adult, I could earn a GED. Once I had that, then I could go for a college degree in something. I wasn't going to jump ahead and think about what my career would be. Nope, getting the GED was first and enough of a first step.

It always gave me a high to drive out to the Santa Fe Community College. The classes in English, the histories, biology, math, and typing were full of adults, usually tired ones. Men and women who had put in a full day's work before picking up their free textbooks and heading to class.

Thanks to the years at the Chicken Ranch, I could pay cash for anything I needed. The money wouldn't last forever, so in a few years, I would have to start earnin' it again. *How* was the only question. I had faith the answer would come, in time.

The fireplace, as the center of my home life, began in October. I could sit for hours in front of it with a hot buttered rum. Through the picture window next to it, I'd watch my neighbors come and go. Actually, I had met and really enjoyed the two guys who lived next door on the left, my first experience with gay partners. The only question I had, but didn't ask, was why did one of them play the female role and the other the male? If both bein' in male bodies was what turned them on, why the contradiction?

However, puzzlin' about my neighbor's sexuality was the closest I got to sex in my new world. Not that I hadn't been hit on. Yes, I loved noticin' how men admired me, but I didn't have any interest in them, yet! Maybe later on. Later when I was workin' somewhere and more comfortable in my new skin. My life now could be described as eat, sleep, movies, dancing, class and study.

With all the textbooks in my life, I didn't look for anything else to read, but one day when I walked past the magazine rack in Smith's Grocery Store, a magazine cover stopped me cold.

There it was, big as Dallas. On the cover of the October 1973 issue of *Texas Monthly*, 'World's Oldest Profession Hits The Road', page 54. The cover showed two pretty girls, with their suitcases, hitchhikin' out of La Grange.

I glanced around before pickin' it up. I didn't open the magazine, but I did buy it. My heart pounded as I hurried out the door with evidence of my previous life in hand.

Not before I was behind locked doors at home did I turn to page 54. The article was written by Al Reinert. Never heard of him.

First I flipped through the pages to see if there was a picture of me anywhere on the 11 pages of the article. None, thank God, but I did look at Jim's. Bless his heart. I lit a cigarette, sat down in my only rocker in front of the fireplace, and began reading.

TRUE CONFESSIONS

On Wednesday, August 1, 1973, the La Grange Chicken Ranch, the Oldest Continually Operating Non-Floating Whorehouse in the United States, was closed down. The Texas Chamber Of Commerce elected to ignore the passage of an establishment possibly older than all its members; and the State Historical Society, equally misfeasant, overlooked the shuttering of the house that slept more politicians than the Driskill Hotel and the Governor's Mansion combined.

You all know about the Chicken Ranch of course. It was just about the first tourist attraction I heard about when I came to Texas. But, then, I came to Texas to be an Aggie, so that explains that. Later on I even learned that there was a town called La Grange nestled somewhere on the outskirts of the whorehouse of the same name.

Hell, I even went to La Grange once. The whorehouse, I mean. Not, mind you, because I had any truly unquenchable perversions that required a trip to La Grange to unleash, but, rather, because I figured that if one was going to be an Aggie, well then, Be An Aggie. The pilgrimage to La Grange sits close to the heart of The Aggie Myth, as central to the catechism as standing at football games and building the Bonfire for the Texas game.

We went on Thursday night when they had the $8 Aggie Special, trekking down in an old Pontiac full of fraudulently-purchased Lone Star and a thousand obscene variants of some drastically original horny Aggie fantasy.

We circled around town for a while, body temperature rising in inverse proportion to the declining stash of Lone Star and the increasing depravity of the fantasy, a deep, twisted well of prurient anxiety gradually filling to the point where no adolescent squeamishness could possibly abort an explosive gusher of Sinful Lust.

How's that for metaphor? Eh? Us Aggies get a three-syllable handicap in this magazine-writin'. In any case, the air went out of the fantasy as soon as we pulled into the Chicken Ranch parking lot and the first person we spotted was a deputy sheriff. He was just there, to help park cars, though, so we proceeded on up to the door where Lilly the black maid – the only black as matter of strict fact (historical accuracy being an important part of article like this) who ever passed the doors of the Chicken Ranch – checked our phony ID's to make sure we were 21 and let us in.

We sauntered into the parlor where we drunkenly introduced ourselves to a half-dozen local farmers, a couple of cross-country truck drivers, and a fellow pilgrim who'd journeyed all the way down from Nebraska – and three young ladies who either worked there or were truck drivers, too, we weren't sure which.

One of the young ladies offered to sell us a Coke for 50 cents, which we declined, and then one of her friends asked us for a quarter to play the juke box, which we cheerfully provided. My friend Richard, who was still trying to decide if they worked there or were just visiting truck drivers, thought he'd break the ice a little by asking one of them if she wanted to dance, which she didn't.

"What's with this dancin' stuff, honey?" is what she said. "Ya wanna do some business here or not?" That's when we decided she must be one of the U.T. coeds we'd heard about.

Pretty soon after that I picked one of the ladies (or she picked me, quite possibly, my recollection being sort of hazy) and we wandered off down the hall to one of the bedrooms. The walls of the room possessed an angularity that bespoke distracted carpentry, all of them covered with irregular splotches of pastel paint, and the furnishings consisted of a bed, a dresser, and a sink, all rather commonplace in appearance and not at all meeting my expectations.

The dresser drawer had been left open to reveal an

intriguing assortment of oils, photographs, and leather goods, but I held firm for the Aggie Special which didn't include any of its contents. Ruthie, who was the lady I picked (or who'd picked me), just rolled her eyes and made a face when I told her I only had the eight dollars anyway. She told me to "Git yer clothes off, honey," and left to go deposit my money someplace.

I thought for a bit about how this wasn't the way we'd planned it on the way down and was consequently a little slow getting undressed, being still garbed in my pants when Ruthie got back. "What's this?" she asked me. "We ain't got all night, ya know."

I apologized for being so slow and took my pants off. She then started poking and tugging at me, "checkin' fer diseases," she said, a bit of foreplay that possessed all the sensuality of my Army physical. Ruthie next threw me down on the bed, took off her own clothes and lay down beside me, and told me that for just eight dollars I didn't get to kiss her.

Pleased that I hadn't brought any more money, we just started pawing and pulling at each other and, next thing I knew, she was on top of me and asking if I was "finished already, honey?" "Well, uuuh…" I said. Then she pulled me up off the bed, washed us both off, and told me to "git yer clothes back on, honey." It had been what's known in the trade as a "Four-get," Get up, Get on, Get off, and Get out.

I met the rest of my cohorts outside, all except for Richard, for whom we had to wait another hour and a half. He'd been so abased at being turned down for his dance that he'd gone and splurged $40 on a lavish degeneracy of sufficient novelty that its graphic description entertained us all the way back to College Station.

A SENTIMENTAL HISTORY OF
AMERICA'S OLDEST WHOREHOUSE

When old Frank Lotto published the first History of Fayette County back in 1902, he wrote, with what must have been a sly snicker to himself, that "The City of La Grange has made a reputation for sociability over the whole state."

It was nicely located for friendly ambience, being sprawled around high limestone bluffs on a parabolic stretch of the Colorado River in that part of Central Texas where the coastal plains begin gently ballooning into a sinuous undulation that goes westering off to the Hill Country. Dense battalions of age-disfigured live oaks, camouflaged in clouds of hanging moss and sentried by towering cedars, occupy the creek and river bottoms while post oak columns skirt the soft green edges of Bermuda Grass hillsides and cypress files demarcate the boundaries of old Spanish land grants. The Second Congress of the Republic of Texas, enticed by vistas "that but few countryes on Earth can compare with," overwhelmingly voted to establish their permanent capital at La Grange, and only President Sam Houston's self-serving veto kept it in the still-unbuilt jerkwater burg named for himself.

If the easy-rolling richness of Fayette County posed no strong attraction for General Sam, it proved a powerful lure across the world in Central Europe. Beginning in the 1830's it became the terminus for South Germans and Bohemians in flight from famine and persecution. They brought with them an industrious capacity for small farming, which still endures, and an independence of mind bordering on the perverse, which also still endures. Ever since 1860, when they voted not to secede with the rest of the state, Fayette County has maintained a strong tradition of political aberrance.

The immigrants also imported a zesty beer-hall enthusiasm for rowdy pleasures. Indeed, nothing in the county's history has proven so consistently unpopular as Temperance, which went down to its first massive electoral defeat in 1877. It was the kind of indulgent tolerance that could sanction the longest-running brothel ever to open its doors and beds in America. Just when exactly those doors and beds did open is a point of some contention. Dates offered range all the way from 1844, based largely on myth, to 1915, when the house was installed in its present location on the outskirts of town. The most likely occasion for its founding is somewhere in between, with several La Grange old timers remembering its definite existence prior to the turn of the century. Ernest Emmerich, who was town marshall in neighboring Round Top back around the First World War, remembers then County Sheriff August Loessin telling him it was there when August took office in 1894.

The debate, in any case, is spuriously academic. Just as a history of North America, despite its prior existence, doesn't really commence until Columbus, so the True Story of the Chicken Ranch doesn't begin until the arrival, in about 1905, of Ms. Faye Stewart, alias Jessie Williams, and known to friends, employees, numerous intimate acquaintances and elusive Posterity as Miss Jessie.

Originally from Hubbard, up near Waco, Miss Jessie was a whorehouse madam on an epic scale, prostitution's answer to Casey Stengel or Vince Lombardi, author and actor in one of the great chapters in the journal of her profession. A woman of undeniable personal resonance, with rough-hewn country charm and shrewd backwoods tenacity, she is still discussed with soft-eyed affection and reverential tones by those who knew her.

Buddy Zapalac, the editor of the La Grange Journal, says, "She just had ta be one a the most amazin' women who ever lived. She was strong! But she was generous, too. And whoooh Boy! But she was a smart one."

It was Miss Jessie who somehow brought discipline and profit to the house while making peace with the surrounding community at large and its power center in particular; she also negotiated the tacit treaties that enabled her house to survive in the face of contradiction and indignation, a diplomatic performance rivaling those of Henry Kissinger.

Among the first allies she acquired were the Loessin brothers, August and Will, the former being County Sheriff and the latter, younger, being at once the City Marshall in La Grange and his brother's chief deputy (and later his successor as Sheriff). Widely venerated as peace officers, the brothers Loessin seem genuinely to have been well-respected and able peace-keepers, August being the only Central Texas Sheriff to crush the Ku Klux Klan during its bloody pre-War resurgence and Will earning a statewide reputation for ingenious detective work.

The early basis for their pact with Miss Jessie seems to have been a kind of mutual coexistence. She foreswore many of those sidelines that would seem natural in a county cathouse, liquor most notably, and operated it as peaceably and businesslike as the Post Office. The two sheriffs, for their part, just ignored it.

It was a beneficial relationship. Miss Jessie prospered and in 1915, she abandoned the battered downtown hotel they then occupied, and moved her business to the southeastern outskirts of town. She brought in a few new girls as well, including two sisters who learned their craft in the break-hell East Texas oil boom and were to serve as middle management. The house was by now rooting itself into the communal fabric of La Grange and its resident employees, encouraged by Miss Jessie to stay on a permanent basis, had fashioned a broad array of links with the townsfolk; when the boys from La Grange went overseas to Save Democracy in The Great War, the girls from the Ranch sent them cookies.

Soon after the end of the war, Will Loessin was elected to succeed his brother. At some nebulous, earlier point he had made a discovery that struck a glorious chord in his detective heart, one that would repercuss down through all the following years of Fayette County law enforcement. This was, in essence, the men, significantly including local lawbreakers, are (1) habitually prone to bursts of braggadocio, often self-incriminating and helpfully revealing, when they are in bed with women, and (2) these same men were regularly inclined to go to bed with women out at Miss Jessie's. Wonder of Wonders! Will Loessin, in one of the grandest strokes in the annuals of detectivery, had buried deep in the twisted solar plexus of the criminal element an incredibly Organic Wiretap.

And Miss Jessie, not disinterested in further cementing her alliance with the forces of justice, was graciously amenable to stepped-up cooperation. From thence forward, continuing on through all of his 26 years as County Sheriff, Will Loessin would journey nightly out to the edge of town to visit with Miss Jessie and learn what intelligence may have been ferreted out by this subtle pack of eavesdroppers.

The Ranch itself was undergoing a little facelift about this time. Not only had Miss Jessie added on a couple of rooms to accommodate her burgeoning flock, but the Gilded Age of post-war ebullience was sending liberating vibrations even unto the outskirts of La Grange. The girls acquired shiny new cars and flapperish regalia, the rooms received new paint and overstuffed furniture, frenetic snatches of jazz were caught drifting through the woods, and Miss Jessie's unpretentious country whorehouse almost became a bawdy citified "sporting house' as it passed through the gaudiest phase of its lifetime.

The emancipation of the Ranch, though, did not include any creatively expanded repertoire of available pleasures. Waco-bred Miss Jessie had always looked with fundamental distaste on all possible erotic combinations that went beyond the dully conventional missionary position, and the continentally-whetted appetites of war-returned farmboys made her furious.

One La Grange oldtimer, a thrice-weekly regular back in those days, remembers trying to explain to a girl named "Deaf' Eddie how to navigate one pleasantly intricate movement: "See, we called 'er Deaf Eddie 'cause she really was harda hearin', so I was havin' ta talk purty loud. Well, whut happened is thet Miss Jessie heard me an come acrashin' inta there hittin' me with a big iron rod and hollerin' 'bout turnin' her girls inta French whores. She throwed me out an' wouldna let me back fer a month."

Prices at Miss Jessie's then were on an easily computed sliding scale based solely on the time consumed, climbing from $3 up to about a $40 maximum, and not until years later did other variables serve to complicate the equation. The only disruption of these simple accounting procedures came with the Great Depression, when rural economies collapsed into a chaos of barter and salvage.

Miss Jessie, whose Depression-sparked social consciousness would make her one of the fiercest New Dealers in the county, promptly adjusted to the new market by accepting payment in farm produce at the straightforward rate of one chicken, one screw. The backyard was quickly over-run with scratching and fluttering Dominickers and Rhode Island Reds, and the heretofore anonymous whorehouse became the Chicken Ranch.

Thus christened, the Ranch passed quietly through the rest of the decade, the only disruptions caused by a rare and foolish Republican who had the temerity to challenge Miss Jessie's estimation of Franklin Roosevelt.

The Ranch was by then thoroughly imbedded in the webwork of life in Fayette County. Miss Jessie contributed money to local civic clubs and church bazaars, establishing the policy of municipal philanthropy that in later years would see the Ranch become the largest sponsor of the Little League. And, while stopping short of joining the Jaycees, Miss Jessie manipulated capital expenditures in a way that best suited everyone, not excluding herself. Deliveries from groceries, hardware stores, dairies, five-and-dimes, all were rotated on a weekly basis so that each would receive their share of the Ranch's business.

Early in his tenure, Will Loessin had begun the tradition, which continued on up to this year, of reporting on conditions at the Ranch to the twice-annual Fayette County Grand Jury. Estimates of revenue, reports on fights or arrests or information learned were all provided, and an occasionally rambunctious Grand Jury would troop on out to see for themselves, Miss Jessie pleasantly showing them around. In later years, girls going to work at the Ranch would stop first at the sheriff's office to be mugged and fingerprinted, so that checks could be run to see if they'd ever done something illegal somewhere.

One of those early Grand Juries began the practice

of requiring weekly medical exams for the girls at Miss Jessie's, and the office of County Medical Examiner was created solely for that purpose. In more modern times, after the office was abolished, the girls would appear every Thursday at the La Grange Health Clinic to have their non-contaminatory status officially certified.

When America found itself in another war in 1941 and a second generation of Fayette County farmboys left to participate, the girls at Miss Jessie's again sent cookies and wrapped bandages for the Red Cross. The army moved in a training center at nearby Bastrop and, apparently concerned that indiscriminate whoring might short-circuit the American soldier's innate killer instincts, launched a wide-ranging campaign against prostitution. Life at the Ranch temporarily became a little more circumspect, the officially subversive operations went unimpaired for the duration.

The end of the War brought, amidst other happenings, the retirement of Will Loessin; his replacement, ascending almost mechanically into the vacancy, was T.J. 'Jim' Flournoy, who had been Will's chief deputy for a dozen years before putting in a stint as a Texas Ranger. In the same inevitable manner that a national administration will assume the accumulated allies and obligations of all its predecessors, Jim Flournoy inherited all those instinctive understandings and tacit pacts that Miss Jessie had forged 40 years earlier with the Loessin brothers; the momentum of the Ranch swept past another milepost without a missed step or a side glance.

Some of that feisty energy that had driven her thus far had begun to subside, though, and, while post-war prosperity was acknowledged in the form of a couple more lacked-on bedrooms, the attendant post-war exuberance inspire no response at the Ranch. They just settled a few years earlier into that semi-moribund inertia that captured the country though most of the fifties.

Miss Jessie, wheelchair-bound in her last years, watched the decade turn from the front porch of the Chicken Ranch, still firmly in command and admitting respect for no one since Franklin Roosevelt. She died, Faye Stewart died, in 1961, mourned by many who were too embarrassed to demonstrate it and missed by four generations of men whose passage from innocence she had administered.

She had, moreover, wrought permanent change in the world she occupied: her Ranch, at some ephemeral point in its passage through the years, had transcended its role as merely a whorehouse to become an Institution, as important a work in the Gallery of Texana as Spindletop or San Jacinto. The Whorehouse at La Grange had passed mouth-to-ear through the locker-room memories of four generations of Texas men, and its widespread acceptance was tacit acknowledgement of its new status.

The Texas Legislature made reference to it in light-hearted floor debate as early as the forties, and Miss Jessie returned the compliment by amending her cash-only policy to include the acceptance of state payroll checks. Books, magazines, and newspapers all wrote sympathetically of its existence and, as the sixties appeared, adventuresome students would make it a topic for term papers and masters' theses.

Indeed, if the Chicken Ranch is viewed strictly as an illegal brothel, then the largest part of the State of Texas was for 20 years involved in a cover-up of unmatched proportions. More likely, the Ranch had passed beyond reach of The Law into another, more sentimental, dimension where The Law serves no purpose.

Miss Jessie was to be succeeded by a woman as thoroughly schooled for her role as Jim Flournoy had been for his. Edna Milton had come to work at the Ranch in 1952, and by the time Miss Jessie died was chief lieutenant in the management of the house. Red-haired and tough-skinned, with clear-green Laser-piercing eyes, Edna evokes an authoritative confidence that could as easily run a Teamsters local as a whorehouse.

She arranged to purchase the Ranch from Faye Stewart's estate and installed herself as madam, moving into the master bedroom that still contained Miss Jessie's massive four-poster walnut bed. To all appearances the house absorbed the shift in management as effortlessly as it had the paper alteration of ownership, the only real changes being the installation of air-conditioning and the offering of a limited variety of 'exotic extras'.

Edna, even before Miss Jessie died, had been in charge when the Ranch weathered its greatest crisis: Texas Attorney General Will Wilson, who wanted to be a U.S. Senator, had sounded the call for a great moral crusade aimed vaguely at making the state safe for the easily outraged, who presumably form an impressive bloc of voters.

State law enforcement officials were dashing hungrily around on the hot trail of sin, very nearly arresting the entire island of Galveston, and it seemed likely that the Chicken Ranch, as the state's most notoriously renowned whorehouse, would be a sure target.

Edna's response was to go underground, making the pretense of shutting down while admitting regular customers through the back door. It was good enough. Like all crusades, Wilson's choked on the heat of its own righteousness and he soon went away. The Ranch slipped back into a normal high gear and went humming along into its future, sweetly indifferent to muffled indignation or pious politicians, prepared to cope when necessary with the inevitable next crusade.

The next crusader, though, would come armed with cameras.

THE ELECTRIC BOUNTY HUNTER
MEETS THE NIGHTMARE SHERIFF

Marvin Zindler was a public curiosity even before he became a nightly refutation of McLuhan's thesis that television is the province of the cool. Marvin is most assuredly not cool, and never has been. Back when he was heading the Consumer Protection Division of the Harris County Sheriff's Department, he would inveigh against truthless advertisers or fast-dealing car salesmen with all the indignant wrath of a Calvinist preacher accosted in the pulpit by some hot-eyed, leering flasher. And always with an audience. Marvin Zindler was to huckstering what Jehovah's God was to sin, with the exception that Marvin always had cameras there to record the pointing of his vengeful finger.

He had a fair penchant for attracting attention. Stories used to float around the city rooms of Houston newspapers about how Marvin would wait two and three days before serving a warrant until a TV crew was available to immortalize his crime-busting; about how Marvin would deluge courthouse reporters with Agatha Christie-style press releases extolling his exploits; about the time The Houston Post, on Marvin's 'hot inside tip' bannered the four-inch headline HARRELSON IN MEXICO at the same moment the accused murderer was being arrested in Atlanta.

Back when he was the police reporter for a Houston radio station, Zindler would appear just before his on-air signal to relate action-packed on-the-scene accounts that he'd just read from the morning papers. Other reporters used to substitute dated papers and he'd dash into announce, over the air, "This is Marvin Zindler, On The Scene...." And launch into a breathless blow-by-blow of last month's liquor store holdups.

Zindler even looks the part, which is to say artificial. His nose and chin were metamorphosed long ago to meet superstar specifications, and his head is permanently hidden by a handsome Cary Grant toupee. And his clothes, equally handsome, are custom-tailored to conceal the pads he wears on his shoulders and buttocks to fill out his figure to superstar proportions.

It's always been easy, of course, to make fun of Marvin Zindler, as do most of his colleagues in journalism. But, strangely enough, it just won't wash. For one thing, he's so absurdly up-front about those wigs and pads and nosejobs of his, and he confesses instantly, cheerfully, to a raging egomania. It's hard to laugh at somebody's closet skeletons when they rattle them at you.

And then there're his eyes, as warmly blue and gentle (and genuine) as any superstar could hope to possess, the only external hint that within that ludicrously handmade body of his there's a soft nub of sincerity and compassion.

Danny, who's sort of a hustler, remembers being arrested by Marvin way back when he was just another deputy in the Warrants Division: "Most of the crooks I know have a lotta respect for Zindler. He was a straight-up cop. After he'd busted ya, he'd stick around till ya were mugged an' printed an' in the tank, an' he'd make sure ya had cigarettes before he'd leave."

He still shows that same concern in his role as Channel 13's consumer affairs reporter, staying long after work to answer a blizzard of phone calls from 12-year-olds with lost bicycles and dowdy matrons who don't like the gas company. He rationalizes his media-mongering by saying, "Most corporations involved in, say, false advertising will just laugh at a $50 fine, but if you show up with a TV camera and give 'em bad publicity then they'll shape up."

There's a hard truth there. If Marvin's style, a zany blend of P.T. Barnum and Dudley Do-Right, has made him notorious, it's also made him effective; instead of being just another petty public ombudsman, he's become a kind of Electric Bounty Hunter, striking Media-Terror into the fast-talking hearts of consumer bilkers.

That's why it all seemed a little strange when Marvin set out after the Chicken Ranch: while there may well be lots of people who don't like the place, irate consumers aren't among them. But Marvin says his crusade against the Ranch wasn't based on any righteous shock at all the whoring going down out there. "I'm no moralist," he'll tell you. Marvin's targets were bigger than just sin: political corruption and Organized Crime.

Marvin's story is that he got his hands on a Department of Public Safety (DPS) intelligence report that had been made last year. This report, according to Marvin, says that the Chicken Ranch – together with another, less reknowned, little whorehouse in Sealy – grosses ' a conservative minimum' of $3 million a year, and that most of this money was going into numbered bank accounts in Mexico by way of lavish payoffs to all manner of corrupt state and local officials. It's the officials, the story goes, who really own the Chicken Ranch and whose power in

Austin allows it to stay open.

Then there's the black specter of Organized Crime, whose ruthless involvement Marvin keeps invoking. Marvin's definition of Organized Crime, though, is not exactly what you'd first think. It has nothing to do with the Mafia. Or the Syndicate. Or Chicago or New York or even Houston. It maybe has something to do with a 'circuit' of other country whorehouses through which the girls are rotated, but it's hard to say. Marvin's definition of Organized Crime is pretty vague.

Nonetheless, Marvin bought this DPS report at face value, lock-stock-and-brothel. He has great faith in the Texas Rangers.

When he first saw the report last January, he says, he was asked by the Rangers not to do anything until they'd had a chance to 'move in'. Marvin agreed. Then, along about May, Marvin got word that the DPS-Rangers investigation had been cancelled. "That's when I really got mad," remembers Marvin, "cause it proved to me that somebody from higher up was interfering with the enforcing of the law."

That's when Marvin went to work. He recruited as his collaborator Larry Conners, a young TV newsman who is a first-rate investigative reporter and the most hard-ass interviewer this side of Mike Wallace. The Zindler and Connors team went underground to begin their investigation.

They sat in the woods outside the Ranch counting and photographing the patrons. Connors, together with a cameraman (but, sadly, no TV camera) handled the 'inside work,' discovering first-hand that there really was prostitution going on in there.

Old Jim Flournoy looks like he leapt full-bodied

from one of Bobby Seale's nightmare visions of a county sheriff, a pot-bellied, gun-totin', hulking incarnation of Frontier Justice. Slow-talking, in keeping with his thought patterns, Big Jim's style of dealing with the world is based largely on Threat, and is generally successful. His brother Mike, who is the sheriff over in Wharton County, has a reputation for carrying out his threats, but big Jim's never gone overboard with that sort of thing.

Like his predecessors, Big Jim was easily accommodated to the existence of the Chicken Ranch. Back in 1958 he'd even had a Hot Line installed to connect the Ranch and the Sheriff's Office, and he's one of the biggest defenders of its operations. "It's nevrah caused no trouble round here," he says, "no fights or dope or nothing. I ain't nevrah got no complaints."

It's been a positive boon to law enforcement, if you listen to the sheriff. Because of the Ranch, "Thar's nevrah been no rapes while I been shurff," he relates. "O course thet don't count no nigger rapes," he adds, which is probably fair enough since blacks weren't admitted to the Ranch anyway.

He goes on to tell you about the $10,000 that Edna contributed to the Hospital Building Fund, her other munificences, the economic benefits to the community, the low rate of venereal disease afforded by having county-inspected hookers on hand. As Larry Connors puts it, "He makes that whorehouse sound like a damn non-profit county recreational facility."

Most of Big Jim's arguments are pretty specious as well. His figures on rapes, VD, pregnancies, and dope (all of which he says there are none of, excepting for niggers) are all bogus, and the $10,000 bequest about equals the annual take on the jukebox. As for the local impact, one local shopkeeper easily dismissed that: "They only got a payroll of a dozen out there. Now how much money you figure a dozen whores're gonna spend in this town?"

All sad but true. For all Big Jim's efforts at rationalizing, the Ranch's longevity was built on sentiment rather than cash, and sentiment is a poor defense against either the law or a zealous camera. Once Channel 13 weighed in against the 'bawdy houses', as they called them, there was no contest.

That doesn't mean, however, that Zindler ever proved his vague assertions about 'corruption and Organized Crime.' He never even proved his contention that the two whorehouses grossed over $3 million a year; most local Ranch-watchers think that ludicrously high and the most commonly accepted figure was about $300,000. The IRS, who never failed to collect the government's portion, never questioned Edna's returns.

All that Marvin had to do, really, was haul his cameras out to La Grange and put on the tube what every local farmboy for a hundred miles already knew.

Big Jim, who'd probably never before seen the business end of a TV camera, was mercilessly pinned in one of those Connors interviews. He erupted against those goddam DPS fellers who'd been poking around last fall, and allowed as how he'd called DPS Chief Col. Wilson Spelt to get them off his back. The Colonel, said Big Jim, told him to close down the Ranch until the elections were over with, so Big Jim obliged. It was the kind of interview that could make you wonder whose side he was really on.

After a week of nightly exposes, during which the Ranch kept whoring along with all flags flying, Marvin went up to Austin to interview the Governor, the Attorney General, and Col. Speir. Confronted simultaneously with prima faecie sin and TV cameras, they all professed outrage that this could be going on and promised to get to the bottom of things.

On Wednesday, the day before he was to go to Austin to answer a summons from the Governor, Big Jim capitulated. He just called Edna and told her to shut it down. Marvin promptly left for Jamaica on vacation.

Within a week of its shuttering, the Ranch is deserted, with only Lilly still hanging around to shoo off curious interlopers. The girls are in Dallas, Houston, Austin, streetwalking. Big Jim is being especially suspicious of strangers, hinting bluntly to the writer from Playboy that he's seen about all the snoopy journalists he cares to.

At Berkelbach's Café in Round Top, the hangers-on discuss what to do with Marvin Zindler should he ever chance to pass through town. A petition circulates in La Grange to save the ranch, and bumper stickers make their appearance, proclaiming the same thing. Local opinion, as figured by the owner of the local radio station, breaks about even. A few local tycoons begin making plans to buy the Ranch and turn it into a restaurant, with private dining rooms in each of the bedrooms.

There is, indeed, little evidence of any sort that the ranch had ended its days. It had always existed, really, as a pleasant irrelevance, kind of a collective daydream by a rural people that believed in dreams remnant from a simpler era that had a tolerant niche for such things, along with eccentric uncles and town drunks. Like all the excess baggage from that era, realized clay dreams have been burrowed under by the plow of progress. X-rated movies and celluloid sex are alright in the modern age – as is everything that is malleable into legalisms and electricity – but that additional dimensions of humanity that the ranch possessed is out of scene, not immoral, just obsolete.

I closed the magazine so my mind could get back to New Mexico from Texas, Shadows had now entered the living room, so I turned on the kitchen light to pour myself a glass of wine. I started a fire in the fireplace and then lit a cigarette. I looked back at the magazine lyin' on the seat of the rocker. I picked it up again and stared at it for a few seconds before gently placing it on the fire. I sat down and watched it burn. Little by little, my Texas past was being transformed into smoke and ashes.

A few seconds passed before I realized I wasn't eaten up with emotion. No drama at all. Had I finally turned the corner on my past? Clearly whorehouses are now a thing of the past. Mine was outstanding. One that was a real part of Texas history.

Fate had played me a wonderful hand. A new life must have been meant for me, and thanks to that TV personality, I now had it. Not my doing and having no clue as to whose it was didn't concern me this fall evening in Santa Fe. I got up and reached for a light wrap. It's a good night for another movie.

Many months passed before I realized the obvious. I loved the classroom. The teacher was in many ways a performer. And they controlled the atmosphere and direction of learning. Determining grades gave them a position of power too.

As I drove home with my newly earned GED on

the front seat, I decided right then and there to be-come a teacher. A high school teacher, of teenagers not little kids. A teacher's certificate in social studies with a minor in English would do.

The calendar read August of 1974. No time like the present to get started. Fall semester would start in September. I'd be there.

I was and I quickly saw that I'm the oldest one in all my classes, and that makes me special. I have the most to say because I am more interested than the twenty year olds, and I make the best grades. The professors like me, too. My years and my hidden life experiences get revealed in my take on discussion topics.

They would all—my classmates and the profs—be shocked out of their pants to learn who I am. Correc-tion, who I had been. It was fun to contemplate, but never was I tempted to share my past with anyone. No one, ever.

Getting my grammar correct and cleaning up my vocabulary were my biggest challenges. Wish I had a nickel for every time I said 'ain't... isn't' or 'shit... oh my goodness.'

Three years rolled by on the largest life I had ever known. Dinner parties with neighbors (when it was my turn, I had one of the many wonderful cafés cater the meal); movie dates with Sandi, a single lady I had met while dancing at Rodeo Nights; day hiking with a small club of hikers; trips to cultural cites like Chaco Canyon, Ghost Ranch, the historic Plaza Hotel in Las Vegas, NM, and the Saint James Hotel in Cimarron, NM, and the Kasha-Katuwe tent rocks national monument.

People on the college staff arranged and guided some of these trips for a reasonable price, even a weekend trip to White Sands. I loved the variety of people who enjoyed these outings with me. Just great social times, nothing personal happening.

My day job was to study and do well in my classes and at night there was no end to entertainment possibilities. Sandi fast became my only real friend. She was an art teacher at Santa Fe High School, so we were already looking forward to our lives together there when I was certified to teach. I loved her energy and it seemed to be limitless. Of course she was seven years younger than me, but our souls were the same vintage. She loved to dance, hike, ski, fish, travel, and date. Divorce had rendered her very selective and cautious, but she did like the social whirl of one guy and then the next. I had trouble keeping the names current. And it was Sandi who invited me to go to church with her before our usual lunch at the Cowgirl and live music on Sundays. I was promised that it wasn't a regular church. In fact the name of it was new to me: Center for Spiritual Living. I decided to go.

What harm could it do? I had gotten tired of Sandi asking me almost every Saturday night when we were leaving Rodeo Nights.

"It doesn't look like any church I've ever seen," I said as Sandi parked across the street from this office-looking building.

Sandi laughed. "I told you it was different. I'm so glad you are finally coming with me. You are one hard nut to crack."

We walked through the door into a lobby crowded with people visiting and drinking coffee. Instantly Sandi was hailed and off she went.

I stood there for a second before a stranger came right up to me and smiled a welcome and gave me a hug before I knew what was happening. I didn't let on, but I didn't really like that much. I forced myself to go on into the church and take a seat. There was nothing churchy about the place.

When the music started Sandi found me and sat down. "You okay?" she whispered.

I nodded my head. I found myself resisting tears and a strong instinct to flee. But not wanting to be conspicuous kept me in my seat and staring straight ahead. The speaker was dressed casually and he was unassuming.

I can listen to anything. I'm here, so I'll listen.

He started by reassuring his listeners that sins are but mistakes made out of ignorance, naiveté, or desperation. He stressed that everyone, including himself, at some time or another makes a mistake of some type. He taught that if the mistaking person pays attention to the consequences of their behavior, there will be valuable spiritual lessons to be learned.

"And what are those lessons?" he said, "but the unquestionable right to be forgiven."

He explained forgiveness comes naturally from one's inherent connection with the Spirit, and will not only cleanse the soul through love, but also will enlighten the mind with wisdom, and thus prevent future mistakes. He concluded his talk by saying, "There is no such thing as an unforgiving God, nor a behavior so foul that cannot be transformed into a hopeful resolution."

We were getting back in the car to drive to Cowgirls for lunch when Sandi said, "Well, what did you think?"

"I don't know. Give me a minute. We can talk about it over lunch."

Sandi gave me a funny look, but said nothing more.

Our favorite table was available and I was grateful for the fact that there were customers who knew Sandi and had her attention. I sat down and wished I was home. I couldn't talk to Sandi or anyone else about the abortion, the sinful desperation thing I was most guilty of.

"So tell me what you think about the idea of redemption." Sandi was seated and ready to talk.

"Sounds hopeful, but I'm not sure."

"Why not?" Sandi peered into my eyes like never before.

"Well, hell. Oops, sorry. How does anyone know God is forgiving of everything?" I couldn't meet Sandi's eyes.

"Same way we know what we know about God. It is in the Bible."

"And who wrote the Bible, but men. Long after Jesus was dead and buried... so to speak."

I could tell Sandi was shocked. She said in a soft voice, "Is that why you haven't wanted to go to church with me? You don't really believe in God or the Bible?"

"I don't know what I believe. Haven't really had any experience with church going. You might say I'm real ignorant on the subject."

Sandi jumped right in. "And I'm real ignorant on the subject of you. How long have we known each other now? Years? And all I know is where you live and that you drove here from Texas. Have you ever been married? Do you have children? What was your Texas life, and do you have any family? You have never said. That isn't just mysterious, but down right aggravating for me. I'm your friend, for goodness sakes." She wasn't smiling.

I saw where this was going and needed to put a stop to it, but without insulting my new friend. I smiled at Sandi. "Nothing much at all to tell. One very brief marriage when I was a kid. No children and no family I keep up with, and working as a waitress was about it. I promise you there is nothing exotic or romantic to know about my past. I'm just so thrilled to be here in Santa Fe and to have you in my life." Obviously my willingness to lie was still firmly in tact.

Sandi smiled when I told her I'd go with her again to church. That ended the subject. The food arrived and the music started. Another perfect Sunday afternoon in The City Different.

And I did. We started going to church together almost every Sunday. Little by little, my silent tears that came from the seat of my soul stopped. A bright light gradually poured from my heart space. I suspected it would take time, but maybe, just maybe, my life was taking an irreversible turn and I was overcome by hope.

Life for me now took on a rhythm that created a secure, known space. I attended class at the college; did homework; went dancing and to the movies and to special events; shopped for groceries, cleaned house and washed my car at the same places and at a usual time.

Sandi and her multitude of friends included me more

often than I really wanted. But for some reason I couldn't explain, my favorite thing was being alone. I was never lonely or scared or depressed. My habit was beginning each day with a cup of coffee in my rocker. I would survey my home and without making a big deal out of it, acknowledge my blessings. Only in rare dreams did I relive the brothel days. And not even Ben came in dreams as he had once. I had escaped my past, or nearly so.

One day grocery shopping in the just-opened Albertsons, someone yanked me back to Texas past life, Santa Fe style. "Pardon me, madam. I'm Michael Brill, a numerologist."

The word 'madam' made me feel sick immediately. "Yes?"

He smiled. "I have noticed you on three different aisles today here in this new store. Whenever this happens to me, I take it as a sign that there is something in your life you want an answer for."

"You want me to ask you a question about my life? Are you serious?" I was more than a little put off.

Again he smiled. "Only if you want to."

Well hell, why not, I reasoned. Something academic. It took me only a second to ask, "What am I to do with my life?"

He nodded. "Give me three single-digit numbers that pop into your head."

Instantly I answered, "One, five, nine."

"One: Have confidence to move forward. Five: Have confidence to deal with changes and transitions that are coming. Nine: Let go of the past. Stop looking over your shoulder and start doing what you love." He handed me his card and said, "Call me if you want more answers."

Before I could open my mouth, he turned away and walked down the cereal aisle.

I planned to throw away his card, but didn't. True, his answers fit my situation, but for how many others too, I reasoned. Santa Fe was notorious for all kinds of unorthodox ways to learn about yourself. But, I hadn't been tempted because of my unwillingness to look at myself in a rear view mirror. Escape was what I wanted, not understanding.

I must remember to tell Sandi about this, was my last thought about the episode, before getting back to my college paper on the way the Nazi Party got control of Germany.

I now drove daily to the University of New Mexico in Albuquerque for my teaching certification. Only two more semesters to go.

———

A year later, as I walked through the door of the Student Center at Santa Fe High School, I saw Michael Brill again. Before I could collect myself he was already approaching me.

"Well, look at you. How long has it been? You stopped buying your groceries at Albertsons because of me?" His laugh was an eruption of joy and flirtation.

I took a good look at him before answering. He was a tall man, but his wide berth made him seem less so. Salt and pepper hair was full and recently assaulted by the wind that lived on the high hill campus. His eyes were sparkling, yet a tad pale blue. A heavy beard left him looking like a lumberjack.

"Well my goodness. Are you a teacher here?" I asked as my heart sped up and my voice took on its nervous sound. I hadn't forgotten our chance encounter at the grocery store, and I was trusting that he couldn't read my mind.

His laugh filled the hall and he was clearly glad to see me. "I teach government in the Academic Building, so I'll be seeing you around."

"How did you know I have just been hired to teach world history?"

"Oh, don't you remember? I know everything!" He laughed again.

I smiled back at him. "Right. I'll keep that in mind."

As I busied myself all afternoon preparing the classroom for my first year as a teacher, I couldn't help but recall how that man made me feel. He was attractive in a rural way, but more importantly, he was interesting.

This was going to be good. It was high time I had some romance in my life and this Michael Brill might just be the ticket. I can't wait to ask Sandi about him.

"He doesn't dance," Sandi said, "and I never see him in town at anything. Probably doesn't have much money. I think he lives way out in the country and here at school he has the reputation of being 'outside-the-box' with his teaching methods and ideas. Why do you ask?"

I could tell by her body language that Sandi wasn't a fan of his. "Oh, nothing special. He has asked me to go hiking with him Saturday and to have dinner at his house."

"Well, for goodness sakes. I've never known you to be interested in a man, so by all means go. How bad could it be? Besides it will give us something besides my love life to talk about."

"Hardly love life, but I will report." I didn't even try to fool myself. I was excited.

Saturday was the usual sunny and September pleasantly warm New Mexico day. As I drove towards Pecos on Interstate 25, I marveled again at the beautiful blue sky that met the red dirt around green mountains. It was such a majestic world. Its beauty tempted me to believe in what folks say about God.

Michael's house was out in the country close to the small pueblo, Pecos. He stood in the open front door like a large oak tree and waved me in. The Native American flute music floated over the sound of the water fountain in the living room. Crystals of all sizes and shapes decorated the room along the walls, hanging from the ceiling and covering crude shelves.

I didn't see any furniture to sit on, but there was a pile of cushions on the rug in front of the fireplace. Incense burned and coffee was waiting. It was only a little after 11 in the morning.

I drank coffee while Michael packed us a lunch. His very old Jeep, he called Jackie, was waiting outside for us. If I had spent any time wondering what I'd have to say to him, the time was wasted. He never stopped talking. He just assumed I was interested to know all about the plant and animal life, so as Jackie scrambled over and around rocks in the non-existent road, I listened.

We would ride a while and then get out and hike to and from Jackie. Only when we were walking did he not talk. Actually, he seemed to leave his body. His eyes took on a vacant look and he didn't appear to be aware of me at all.

Lunch was a mega sandwich and water. The afternoon hours rolled by in a slow haze. It felt to me like we were alone on the planet. No cars or people like on the hiking trails around Santa Fe.

Whenever I felt like it, I would just stop and sit down to stare into the vast high desert space. Michael never interrupted me. Instead, he would show up and sit down to wait until I was ready to go.

On the way back to his house, he said, "I'll pour you a glass of wine and I want you to sit on the porch and watch the sun go down. I'll make us dinner."

There was a chair on the uncovered porch, so I did as I was told. It felt so good to be left to soak up the changing sky as it went from late afternoon to twilight. While I sipped the wine and watched, I felt the insignificance of being a human in the universe. Actually, my past is inconsequential. I'll be a fool if I don't let it go.

By the time dinner was over and the dishes put away, I learned Michael had been a teacher for a long time. However, according to him, this was not his destiny. His plan was to become a world-famous numerologist, author books on the subject, and lecture worldwide.

From listening to him talk, I couldn't help but notice he had a sense of entitlement from Spirit, his word for God. He kept saying, "Order what you want and expect it to arrive."

As I drove home after a 'thank you-good night' light kiss, I thought about that. I had wanted Ben desperately and he hadn't arrived. Next time, I decided, I'll have to challenge Michael on that theory.

I had certainly been right about teaching. It was absolutely the best life I had ever lived. My classroom was my kingdom. The teenagers, my audience. History, my calling. I think I must have been what is known as a 'natural'. No one told me to stand at the door between classes to greet the kids. I even shook hands with them. No one told me to throw in 'off-the-subject' stories that could relate to the lesson. I didn't know what teachable moments were, I just used them. And I honestly liked living around teenagers. They were such a contrast from the adults in my Texas life.

They liked me too. When I would jot little personal notes to them in their journals, they would write me back. They also accepted my way of teaching. Dates, places, names, events were not my emphasis. Instead, I liked to group them into small numbers and give them a scenario to live that related to what we were studying, and then present it to the class at large.

There was one that especially challenged them. Until 1991 when I retired, I used it every year. Eventually, their parents even knew about it, but they sure didn't know how or why it originated.

Every school year, by the time my classes were into the second week of learning about World War II, everyone readily agreed the Nazis were the bad guys. It was an easy progression for the teens to include the German people in their condemnation.

So one time I finally decided it was time for an assignment that would force the students to 'walk in their shoes.' I was sitting in my rocking chair staring at the fireplace one cold Wednesday evening when I got the germ of an idea that I built on. I would divide the class into German families and give them a life situation to deal with. The student families would play their roles in a scripted presentation for the entire class. Following each production, the audience/class would be allowed to approve or challenge the family's solution to their problem.

A GERMAN FAMILY'S CHOICE –
"Can morality be a blanket judgment of
right or wrong?" group production and presentation.

It is November 1944 in Germany. The war effort is going badly and the German people are now being bombed and are hungry and afraid for their lives. All able-bodied men are gone and even the teenage boys. It is very cold and there isn't enough food or fuel.

This family lives in a rural village that is only important because the train runs through it. There are no jobs to be had. Seldom do you see a man who is capable of working. For a couple of months now, there has been some mysterious construction going on out a few miles from the village. The villagers are hopeful it will mean employment for the women and few men who live there. Life is hard. Little children are close to starving. Mothers spend their days trying to find something to cook and keeping their houses warm from the bitter winter.

A father has been returned from the army because of a combat injury. The mother is frail and suffers from depression. Their ten-year-old son spends his days looking for firewood and food in garbage cans. The old woman is the husband's mother. She is too old and weak to do anything other than mend clothes. She sits by the fireplace saying almost nothing. Her hands move the needle. She is always cold.

One day, excitement takes over the drab house when the husband comes home with news that the new plant outside of town is opening and they are hiring. He will go tomorrow to apply and he suggests his wife goes, too. For the first time in months, there is hope for something to eat besides thin potato soup.

It vanishes the next morning when they line up with most of the other villagers. Everyone wants to work. There won't be enough jobs. And the job is... herding people from the trains to the 'plant' where they are stripped of their clothing and gassed to death. Some workers will be in charge of getting them to strip by telling them that they are going to be bathed. Others, marching them into the gas chambers and locking the door. Others, removing gold teeth and hair from the dead bodies. Others, stacking the bodies for burning and then doing it.

The stunned and stone-faced villagers are given overnight to decide and return. Not all of them will be hired because all are not needed. The salary is a decent one. With both a husband and wife working there, money would no longer be a major problem.

The villagers walk back to their homes in silence. No one looks at another. The loud silence is full of distress, anguish, and wretchedness. Doors close and the adults are inside their Spartan houses to decide. The dinner table conversation is about nothing else.

THE ASSIGNMENT: Each member of the family forms an opinion as to what to do. It is shared at dinner and then the father makes the final decision.

This was my favorite way of teaching. I loved sitting back and watching the students play a part to put forth their opinions. Sometimes I had to intercede when the class discussions erupted into passionate vying for the floor.

Never, year after year, was any one family all agreeable to the decision made by the father. Predictably the grandmother would offer, "Death isn't the worst thing that can happen to you." The mother would be unwilling to watch her child die of starvation. The young boy would be in favor of taking the job because his youth would make it impossible for him to predict its effect on his parent's mental health. And if his dad didn't, someone else would. Most often the father would reason that no people would be saved by his sacrifice. His family would starve to death and it would be for nothing.

Once in a while a student noted that the future can't be known. Maybe the war would be over before the family starved. Seldom, but it did happen, a student ventured that desperation in life makes morality a nonissue. When that did occur, I had to rein in my reaction. My inclination was to jump up and down screaming, 'Yes'!

Over a year passed of dinners at my house or at Michael's before we became lovers. The first time was at his country house, which he had decorated in an unusual way.

I always felt like I became a part of some other reality when I was in his house. The hall was a black space with planets and galaxy stars painted on it. The bathroom was a green garden. Around the oversized tub was an abundance of real green plants and fat candles. After my nice long soak with a glass of red wine, while mood music played, Michael performed his famous massage. Naturally, I welcomed going from friend to lover.

His lovemaking was skilled and effective. My enjoyment was his focus. He was a master lover and his pleasure was in direct relation to mine. It was a totally new experience for me, and I loved it. He led and I followed.

Not for one second did I fall back into 'the whore who knew how to play a stranger.' Now, even sexually, I could be different. Honestly, that might have been the best part.

"I take it you're okay?" He asked the question, but he knew he didn't have to. That, 'I'm the man' look on his face said it all. He was proud of his performance and I answered with a smile and lowered eyes. He will never know who he just had in his bed. Lord, wouldn't he just about die? A famous Texas madam enjoying his skills. What a hoot!

Of course, the Ben experience couldn't be matched or forgotten, but at least now I could enjoy a man sexually. I decided to spend the night and loved curling up close around his large, warm body. After coffee the next morning I drove home in the bright New Mexico sunshine thinking, 'no more goddamn days for me.'

And it was Michael who told me about Yelapa, Mexico. His cubby office space was located across the aisle from mine in the social studies department, so often we had time to visit.

On a very snowy Friday in February of 1978, the subject of spring break came up. He couldn't go this year, but he highly recommended this peninsula off the coast of Puerto Vallarta. According to him, the woman's resort there was the nearest thing to heaven he had ever experienced: Isabel Jordan's Casa Isabel.

"It's a good day for some chili, so why not come by the house on your way home to eat. I want to hear all about Yelapa."

"Sounds good," Michael said. "I need an hour or so to finish up here so go on home and make a fire in the fireplace and warm up the chili."

Later that evening as Michael helped himself to more chili, I said, "So what makes Yelapa so special."

"Lord, where do I begin? For starters you walk everywhere you go. No cars. You only get there by boat, and then you can ride a horse or donkey or walk. The trail into town from Isabel's is a narrow path along the edge of the sea. It passes over creeks, huge rocks and around trees. Takes about fifteen minutes, but it isn't steep or hazardous. You just need good balance to get over the rocks in the creek. Once you get into the village, you find your way by wandering the narrow streets that go around and around. No street signs so you just have to memorize which way to go. There are two grocery stores and one little shop on the outskirts that the visiting gringos call the 7-11. Four or five locals sit there around the clock, drinking beer. You will be amazed at the number of cafés, and they are all wonderful. And the margaritas. You will never drink another margarita like you will find in Yelapa."

I was trying to picture a place with no cars, stoplights, or street signs. And walking? I'd have to walk everywhere I went. "I don't know, Michael. Are you sure it is a place for me?"

"It is heaven, absolutely heaven. The beauty of the white beach around deep blue sparkling water, the tropical flowers—along with all kinds of fruits growing wild, and the smiling little brown people—just transport you to another level of consciousness. The place forces you to stay in the moment, if for no other reason than to pay attention to where you put your feet. Horse and donkey caca is in the people path. You will love it."

I moved from the table to the fireplace and lit a cigarette. "Who in the hell lives in such primitive circumstances in the 20th century? What do they do with their lives?"

"Edna, I understand there were early international settlers who built some of the mansions that are used today for resorts. In the 1960's, icons such as Candace Bergen, Bob Dylan and Jack Nicholson were regulars in Yelapa, and Peter Fonda anchored with big black sailboat in the bahia every year. Too, Yelapa has been a vacation spot for Mexican movie stars and TV personalities because they love not having to worry about the paparazzi hounding their families and friends."

I thought about Michael's description for a second or two before saying, "In other words Yelapa is a vigorous, physical experience where I'd go to sun, swim, read and rest. I'd have the opportunity to escape my usual world to be alone with myself. Nights without TV or movies. Instead there are long nights with little between you and nature. I'll meet an interesting assortment of people from all over and dance at the Yacht Club on Saturday night, only if I am willing to walk the trail back to Casa Isabel's with the help of a flashlight."

Michael smiled and stood up to get his jacket. "Absolutely, you got it. Hope you decide to trust me on this and go. You will never regret it."

One week of tropical forest on the Pacific Coast sounded wonderful, so I went. Thus the beginning of an annual spring break trip for me every year until I retired. Isabel and her world were balm for my spirit. Sitting still with myself in nature slowed me down. I could sleep for up to ten hours at a time; I visited with the other guests on the beach; I always found the perfect book to read in Isabel's extensive library, and with a group I even made it to the dances on Saturday nights.

When I first arrived in Yelapa by water taxi from Puerto Vallarta, I saw with my own eyes a Yelapa where almost nothing rolled. No cars, just like Michael said.

The very first time I laid eyes on Isabel, she was seated at the dining table with a friend, drinking a margarita. I was huffing and puffing from the straight-up-from-the-beach steps to Casa Central (the main house for Isabel's business). Since there are no floor-to-ceiling walls at Casa Isabel, I could see her blue-green eyes before I could hear her voice.

As I stepped into the kitchen area of the large one-room kitchen, dining, living room, and library space, she looked up at me and smiled. My reaction to her strong, unwavering gaze was to feel like, with her one glance, she knew me completely. Needless to say, this put me off a bit.

She called me by name, smiled, and invited me to sit down and have a drink with them. I did and it was smooth sailing from that moment on. We walked into the village for dinner at Pollo Bollo, a busy, noisy cantina where the food was really good.

Isabel knew everyone and everyone knew Isabel. We joined a large table of ladies who were staying at Casa Isabel to attend the Compassionate Listening Workshop scheduled for the next day. Linda Wolf, the facilitator, invited me to join them.

Later, as I lay in my moving-with-the-breeze bed (hung from the ceiling to avoid scorpions), I reviewed the travel day and my introduction to Isabel and her casa. Michael was certainly right to think I would relate to this place. Never had I been in a jungle world with the sound of the waves hitting the rocks on the beach, and nothing between me and whatever the night might bring into my *palapa*.

Per Isabel's suggestion, I slept with my flashlight. An open-air palapa has no doors or complete walls.

The night noises were many and strange, but for some reason I was not afraid. I drifted off and slept, without any evidence of moving, until mid-morning.

But some mornings I'd be up and sitting on the patio to watch the sun come up over the blue water. This place could be heaven, I decided, as I stretched and waited for my coffee to make.

Seventy-year-old Isabel was a little more tired than usual this March day. Because of all the guests at Casa Isabel, and the added work of hosting the Compassionate Listening Workshop, she was only now—while taking a hurried shower and dressing—thinking about what to say to the women gathered and expecting her sage words. She was scheduled to be the main speaker at the end of the day.

Maybe I can broach the subject of marriage, Isabel thought, as she selected her favorite earrings. Probably all of the women are or have been, and it certainly qualifies as a topic of universal interest.

"I hope that book by Alain De Botton is still by my bed," she mumbled to herself. "If I remember correctly, he and I share the same views on the subject. I love what he said about it being time for the need for sex and the need for love to be granted equal standing, without an added moral gloss."

Isabel sat down on her bed. "There it is, right where I left it. And when did I start talking to myself?" Isabel wondered, as she thumbed through the book. I don't have much time to decide what I'm going to say. Life on the hurry-up.

A few minutes later, Isabel joined the group, just

reassembled after the last break of the day.

Isabel nodded and smiled. Thankfully she felt her weary bones respond to the energy of the women. The older I get, she realized as she greeted them, the more I prefer the company of women. I'm thinking a preferable arrangement would be to have a woman's mind in a man's body. But I better not say that, was her last thought before she took her place to speak.

"Greetings, ladies. Get comfortable and lets talk a bit about marriage. Do I have any takers?"

I smiled and nodded my head in agreement as did all the other ladies. The sun was going down and a cool breeze off the ocean made me very comfortable, yet alive with the realization that all gathered were fully present with each other and themselves.

"Let me begin with a question," Isabel said, as she smiled at the group of women who were waiting for her to begin. "Who here realizes that modern marriage is very different from its historical precedents?"

I surprised myself by answering right away. "History shows that arranged marriages have been the norm until very recently. The idea of love and individual choice had nothing to do with it."

Isabel's electric eyes fixed on me. "True, nowadays we choose for ourselves. However, that is not what has created the major difference. No, what distinguishes modern marriage from its historical model is its fundamental principle that all our desires for love, sex and family ought to exist in the selfsame person. No other society has been so demanding or so hopeful about the institution of marriage, and as a consequence, so disappointed in it."

A thoughtful silence reigned for several seconds before she continued. "Think about it. How smart is it to insist that one person be all things to you? And why is it that when we are in a relationship, there is no such thing as a minor detail?"

Again I spoke first, but with a question, not an answer. "Are you saying that my idea of a happy marriage is a myth? That a husband be the love of my life, provide well for me, and be a wonderful father—isn't a realistic expectation?"

My memory flew to Ben. I had always believed I would have had it all, married to him. Love, protection, security, family, and more love. I had never questioned these expectations around life with Ben. The life that didn't happen because he died. This was certainly a new thought to ponder, so I did, while waiting for Isabel to answer me.

"It is a possibility, but a very, very rare one. There are three golden strands of fulfillment in marriage: romantic, erotic, and familial. Each affects and hurts the others in unfortunate ways. Nevertheless, I personally think we can guard ourselves against how chaotic and misleading our feelings can be. Our unhappy feelings that can come to surround our marriages are, I think, the result of how we set ourselves up for failure."

"And how do we do that?" A beautiful young woman said, with fire in her eyes. "Give me an example of what you mean. Don't just make an assertion and leave it at that."

Isabel smiled. "Okay, fair enough. Let's take wedding

vows as an example. Instead of the love, honor and obey version, let me suggest something more depictive of life as a couple."

She moved over to the edge of the patio and said to the ocean, but loud enough for all to hear. "What do you think? Would these wedding vows make a difference in how we react to our mate in all the coming years that follow the honeymoon?"

She turned to face the group. "I promise to be disappointed by you and only you alone. I promise to make you the sole storehouse of my regrets, rather than to distribute them widely through multiple affairs or marriages. I have contemplated the different options for unhappiness, and it is you I choose to commit myself to."

No one spoke. I gazed down at my hands, and the silence was filled with reactions no one there could express.

I squirmed in my chair. Those few awful months as Red's wife didn't qualify as a marriage, and I never got to marry Ben. And becoming a wife at this late date, probably not. So I said nothing and no one else did either.

The day was on the verge of ending and Isabel was done. Responses weren't necessary. Individual time to mull over private thoughts was what we could all do with the evening.

So Isabel sat down and looked out to sea as she spoke to me in a low voice, "Please remember that whenever you feel an all but irresistible desire to flee from your thoughts, you can be quite sure there is something important trying to make its way into your consciousness. Don't run. Pay attention." These words sounded like a benediction.

That week, like the many that followed it year after year, was always a time of reflection for me and it didn't matter how easy or challenging life was in Santa Fe at the time. My spring break at Isabel's in Yelapa became a requirement for my soul. I learned to jot down some of the wisdom that poured forth from her for further consideration when I was back home living my life as a teacher.

If she wasn't genuinely interested in helping all others and me with their lives, she fooled me. Our last conversation the night before I came home from that first trip was one that gave me considerable pause. Naturally I never confessed to Isabel my life story, but she must have somehow known I needed to give up my past more completely because she asked, "Edna, have you noticed that people cling to their misery?"

I couldn't keep the irritation I instantly felt out of my voice, "Some people have a shit load of misery, so what do you mean – cling to?"

Isabel thought a minute. "I don't know. It just seems like with misery you have something to do. With the misery, some occupation. With the misery you can avoid yourself. You are engaged. You are the prison. You are the prisoner and you are the one who has imprisoned you."

"Give me an example of what you mean," I asked with no irritation and more respect.

Isabel said, "Most everyone around here knows my daughter Susan died when she was only 21 years old. I had only recently found her after giving her up for adoption when she was born."

I was immediately sorry I had asked, but Isabel gave me a sad smile before she spoke again. "I was destroyed by her death. I spent years carrying around the questions. Why? What was the point? What had I done to deserve this tragedy? How could I ever be happy again?"

Isabel then became silent, and I was uncertain as to what to do. Sit and wait? Offer some condolences? What a dope I am to think I have a monopoly on misery.

"It took me a long while, but I finally got it. You see, Edna, we live every moment of our lives in the solitude of our minds. However close we may be to others, our pleasures and pains are ours alone. Susan's death wasn't causing my misery. I was, by keeping it utmost in my mind. Susan had died once, but I had her dying day after day, year after year."

With sudden tears in my eyes and total understanding, I said, "Me, too. I have done the same thing. The only man I ever loved didn't come back for me. He was killed in the war and the life we had planned didn't happen. The misery of that has never completely left me, although I am happier now than I have ever been since Ben, and what you have said helps me realize I have done it to myself."

I always returned from spring break in March every year with wonderful Isabel and Yelapa stories for Michael. The longer he and I were friends, the more I could relax around him and be myself. And like with Sheriff Jim, he too loved to talk. Numerology was his favorite topic.

For the first several months, he only offered academic

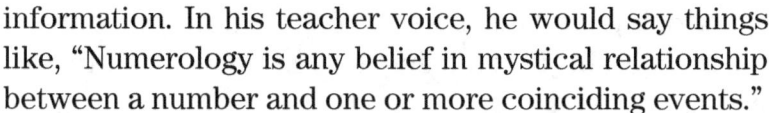

information. In his teacher voice, he would say things like, "Numerology is any belief in mystical relationship between a number and one or more coinciding events."

And his favorite generalization was, "Math is the language between worlds and galaxies."

So, of course, I finally let him 'do the numbers' on me via my full name and birth date. I even paid him to do it because I knew it took time and effort.

On a late Saturday morning, over coffee at his dining table, he produced this one sheet of paper that was a combination of blue, pink and green numbers— one through nine—under headings: life challenges, soul's urge, expression, achievement number, destiny. The triangle shapes designated work, relationships, and family. The one square on the cluttered white paper was labeled personality, with many lines with arrows joining them.

I couldn't help but smile to myself knowing that if I listened to Michael explain all this, I'd probably be on information overload. And sure enough, a few minutes into his explanation I had to interrupt him.

"Michael. Stop, stop, stop. Just tell me the bottom lines. What the different numbers mean and how you arrived at them, I don't need to know. I can't absorb all that information and it just makes me tired to listen to it. I trust you know what you are doing, so you don't need to explain how you arrived at what the numbers say. Just tell me what they say. Okay?"

"Oh, all right, I'll just tell you the positive and negative aspects of your numbers and not bore you with the 'how-come' of the numbers. Is that what you want?"

"Don't pout, Michael. It is too much information for me to digest by just listening to you. I am very interested, go on."

So he continued, "Your number is a 7. Issues involve trust, skepticism, and control. Positive aspects are: trusting, spiritual, analytical, psychic, introspective, empathetic, objective, a seeker of knowledge. Negative aspects are: controlling, fearful, non-trusting, impatient, a need to be needed, totally disconnected emotionally, a martyr. Is that the way you want it?"

I was instantly hooked. "Good grief. Yes, I guess so. Keep going. You certainly have my undivided attention."

He went on, "Okay then, a little more about expression or destiny. The hallmark of the number 7 is a good mind, and especially good at searching out and finding the truth. Very little ever escapes your observation and deep understanding. You can make a very fine teacher. You are very logical and usually employ a quite rational approach to most things you do. At full maturity, you are likely to be a very peaceful and poised individual. The chief negative of 7 relates to the limited degree of trust you may have in people. You are not very adaptable and you may tend to be overly critical and intolerant. You really like to work alone, at your own pace and in your own way. You neither show or understand emotions very well."

I didn't know what to do with my thoughts so I lit another cigarette. Every damn word rang true to me. The good and the not-so-good. I'm some kind of person by virtue of numbers associated with my name and birth. What the hell?

Michael got up from the table to get another cup of coffee. "You want me to go on?"

"Absolutely. Honestly, to say this stuff is interesting is an understatement. For sure, go on. I'm all ears."

Michael sat down and picked up the messy white sheet of paper again. "Your soul urge number is a 1. Its issues have to do with ego-self. You want to lead and direct, to work independent of supervision, by yourself or with subordinates. You take pride in your abilities and want to be recognized for them. You are very attainment oriented and driven to success. However, a negative 1 is apt to dominate situations and people. Emotions aren't strong in this nature. You must avoid being too critical and impatient of trifles. The great need of the 1 is to develop a sincere interest in people."

"Just give me a minute," I said. "I won't remember all this so I need to jot it down. Drink your coffee and let me take some notes."

"Only one more thing today and then your time is up," Michael teased. "Your inner dream number is a 6, which means you dream of guiding and fostering the perfect family in the perfect home. You crave the devotion from offspring and a loving spouse. You picture yourself in the center of a successful domestic unit."

"Stop right there!" I stared at my notes, but I didn't write anything. No way would I forget what Michael had last said.

After this first official session, Michael reserved his numerological comments about me for impromptu moments when they fit with what was happening. For instance, after a lovemaking session when I reached to light a cigarette, he said in his most sage voice, "Your excessive smoking is related to a family dynamic."

"Good to know," I smiled and felt in a good mood. "What else are the numbers telling you tonight?"

Michael rolled over to turn off the lamp on the bedside table. "Control is everything to you. You have feelings but you won't let them come up. You really hate a liar, but you lie at the drop of a hat. You can't really trust because life has taught you that nothing lasts. You fear rejection and you lack self esteem."

I finished my cigarette. The sound from the water fountain in his bedroom was soothing, and I needed that. I wondered if knowing all this about myself would help me change. I doubted it because knowing and changing are two different things.

When I put out the Camel and lay down beside the silent Michael, I grinned in the darkness. "This becoming a student of myself might be more than I bargained for. I was only going for a change of career, lifestyle, and geography."

"Nah! Edna, you're doing great. There is no timetable and no test to pass. No one on this planet is perfect. Sure hope you aren't trying to be. Come here and wrap your sexy body around my fat one. It's cold outside and a great time for a long winter's nap."

———◦———

At the end of May, the close of another school year needed to be celebrated. Michael wanted to be in charge and that was fine with me. A road trip in his old jeep Jackie up to Colorado where we could camp out and enjoy some natural hot springs was the plan. He had friends in the area and too he could do some readings for people for some extra money. Everything seemed to fall into place when we drove out of Santa Fe.

The sign read, "Clothing optional." Immediately, I was irritated as hell. I could feel my flushed face and no doubt Michael noticed my narrowed eyes. No way would I be naked in a public bath. I didn't allow myself to think about why not. Nevertheless, flashes of my nude body and all those of different men forced their way into my mind and ended my good humor.

After setting up the tent, we headed for the natural hot springs where I was right away upset by the variety of humanity in and around the pool. The young attractive ones had on bathing suits. The old, fat, skinny, gray, ugly ones were buck-naked.

As I kept to myself along the side of the pool, I considered my anger. How many men had I seen without their clothes? How many times had I taken mine off in front of strangers?

In his birthday suit, Michael tried to talk to me, but I shooed him away. I was miserable so I kept my head down facing the side of the pool. I couldn't stand the idea of looking at anyone, and it didn't take me too long to get why that was.

Emotionally I was thrown back into my earlier life with just the show of naked bodies. Having on a bathing suit made me a hypocrite. I couldn't get out of there fast enough. I threw on my jeans and almost ran through the meadow to the woods in the distance.

I finally had to stop to sit down. Tears came and all I could think of was William Faulkner's quote in my English textbook: "The past is not dead, it's not even past."

Michael seemed his usual self without a trace of interest or responsibility for my mood. The night passed in silence and without any passion for anything but sleep. He was busy with clients all the next day and that was a good thing. I didn't have to inflict myself on him or anyone else. I avoided the pool and instead took the book I was reading, The Sacred Cows Are Dying by Art Greer to the hay meadow where I spent the day reading, eating my sandwich and pondering the author's words. For example: "We don't change much by ignoring reality."

I closed the book after reading, "Growth and Change and Disturbance and sometimes Discomfort. You ain't ever going to live happily ever after. Sorry."

I gathered up my lunch mess and the old shirt I had sat on. Tonight I'd have dinner in town and get to meet Michael's friends. Enough 'stirring the pot' for one day.

I could not believe it. Was he actually going to ignore my sitting there in the booth with him? His friends, who had joined us, looked at me and then at him, but Michael was oblivious to the need to introduce me.

Finally I spoke, "I'm Edna. I teach with Michael." And the evening went downhill from there.

I attacked him the minute we got back in Jackie. "You are ashamed of me?"

"What in the hell are you talking about, Edna?" He used a new voice.

"You didn't introduce me. You left me sitting there

feeling you were ashamed of me. You fuckin' didn't introduce me." And it felt good to say 'fuck.'

"Are you out of your mind? Ashamed of you? Where did that come from? Is it out of the same box as getting upset because there were some nude bathers yesterday? A couple of blasts from your mysterious past, maybe? And why not add the rub that I never say I love you when we are having sex? You are looking for reasons to break up with me. Fine, honey, you have them."

The next day we drove all the way back to Santa Fe in surprisingly comfortable silence. Michael was no longer mad and neither was I. The day was beautiful and I spent my time thinking about the summer ahead. Sleeping in; reading something other than student essays; dancing downtown at the plaza with tourists and locals; following Sandi around her social calendar; day trips all around Santa Fe.

Absolutely no goddamn days, just Land of Enchantment summer days. I'd see Michael when school started again in the fall and that would be soon enough.

As the school years rolled by, I became more and more involved with the extra-curricula activities. If ever a chaperone was needed, the kids knew where to find me. The Sadie Hawkins dance with all the thumping and jumping music, and the Junior Senior Prom were the biggest nights of the year. They were always in May and usually at the Sweeney Convention Center.

I loved seeing my students in formals and tuxedos. It made me feel special too when the boys asked me to dance. Ernest, one of the Hispanic boys who struggled to stay in school, was there. After we danced, he said in all seriousness, "Miss Milton, if I graduate, will you marry me?"

"Absolutely!" I smiled. If only he doesn't drop out. He is so smart. He could go far. So many of the students don't even have parents in their lives. They couch surf and live on the streets. And under those circumstances, what teenager is motivated to study?

I also got involved with Mr. Ertmer's annual Medieval May Fair. His western civilization class was responsible for the living history where students manned food booths, served as strolling troubadours, lords and ladies. I wasn't the only teacher to get involved. Frank Lembo, the English teacher, portrayed Geoffrey Chaucer.

And then there was the Demon Vaudeville in the spring. I loved helping with this Student Council sponsored talent show. By the time I retired in 1991, teaching a Charleston dance routine became a physical test of my stamina.

Sandi was retiring also and looking forward to becoming an art therapist. And she planned to write children's books. The years had not changed the fact that she was totally an energizer bunny. She could hike all day and dance all night. If only she could sleep. How many times did our conversation revolve around 'sleep'? Sandi tried everything, but it would appear that insomnia was her cross to bear.

I didn't yet have a plan for my retirement years. My health was good and a full life kept me moving, but I did know I would need some other interest to get me out of bed in the mornings.

One Friday, an article in the Pasa Tiempo covered

the need for volunteers to help at the Esperanza Shelter in Santa Fe. I could probably talk to those women, but it would mean drawing on my past. That very same Texas life I have worked so hard to forget. But, of course, if it takes one to help one, then I'm qualified. Maybe...

Instead, I got sidetracked. Michael had moved to Thailand and now I was missing that male interaction. But I decided to do my shopping around for dates online instead of going to the Friday Single Club gatherings. Sandi assured me the pickings weren't so good.

The first two dates were a disappointment, but not the third. Only one question. How could this man be nothing I would order from the menu, and yet get my attention and keep it?

I was early, naturally, so when he walked up to the café in downtown Santa Fe, where we were to meet, I was disappointed to see he was short. Well, actually, my height, but to me, that is short for a man.

I loved his voice, but hated his mustache. From the Bronx in New York, his vocabulary and pronunciation sounded a bit foreign. But he was such fun. He jumped right into telling me his life history with funny asides to match most of the facts.

Clearly Tony Valenti's charm was a combination of his wit and tongue-in-cheek faultfinding. I hadn't laughed so much in ages and by the time he walked me to my car, I had decided he was tall enough.

Tony was legally separated from a 25-year marriage, so he was new to the dating world and making a life for himself. I sprang right in with both feet. He needed help decorating the townhouse he had just purchased, and since he was conditioned to being a couple, my constant company. Our weeks became a combination of shopping for and working on the townhouse and weekend road trips all around northern New Mexico.

He stayed with me once in a while, but usually it was more likely I stayed at his place. We loved to walk down to the plaza to listen to the live summer music. Oh yeah, he didn't dance and that was a major minus. I had always maintained I couldn't love a man who didn't dance and here he was.

He and Michael were nothing alike, and that was, for most purposes, a good thing. Tony was very social so we went to listen to jazz bands in Santa Fe; we had dinner parties at his townhouse; we went to Las Vegas and the Grand Canyon as tourists; we went to the Lensic Theatre to enjoy lectures; we drove out into the rural areas for his photography interests; we spent nights in historical hotels all over New Mexico, and we went to many of Santa Fe's finest restaurants for memorable meals.

Tony introduced me to dirty martinis made with Bombay Sapphire Gin. Then he teased me by saying he was gonna have to take out a loan to keep me liquored up.

He loved Yelapa, too. We went three times together and each trip was better than the last one. Honestly, we could sleep ten hours straight with the sound of the surf hitting the rocks below our palapa. The room offered a double bed with a mattress that sank in the middle, so we just slept without moving for hours on end.

One night he must have been awakened by my struggle to get out of the bed and untangled from the mosquito net covering it and down the narrow trail to the outdoor toilet. Finding a place to shine the flashlight on me while I got myself together, and then the filling of the bucket with water to flush it before retracing my path back inside the palapa, without stepping on a scorpion.

As I lay my head back on my pillow in exhaustion, he whispered, "Piece of cake."

No doubt all the neighbors heard my roars of laughter. That was Tony. Full of funny quips and tall tales. If only he had not been agnostic. At least, that is what I came to blame it on after almost three years.

The more I did volunteer work with the women at the crisis center, the more I couldn't ignore my personal tendency to find fault with the man in my life so I'd have reasons to end the relationship. I saw my pattern. I would hear myself hold forth on some woman's crisis with her husband and then as I drove home, wonder how I could be so dishonest.

After all this time, my life was still more fiction than truth. Ultimately the last thing I was capable of was admitting any fault, great or small. Yet I volunteered at the center for the purpose of being some help to unfortunate women. How is that for irony? It was only last week…

"It is my marriage. As you know, Miss Milton, he drinks too much and I am tired of being abused," began the sad, middle-aged Hispanic woman. Her name was Paz and she was new to the center.

I had been given the assignment of trying to help her with her life. "Paz, you must leave that man," I said quickly and with force.

Paz hung her head and said in a soft but firm voice, "I

can't. Where would I go?"

I looked at her for a long time. "Okay, then I'll help you to stay."

Paz had tears in her eyes, but a faint smile on her face. "You tell me and I'll do it."

I motioned to the couch. "Lie down, close your eyes, and listen to me."

Paz laid down on her back and folded her arms across her face. I sat on the other couch and with, 'Help me God' as my prayer, I began.

"Paz, we teach people how to treat us. You have been married for many years now and your husband knows he can behave badly without any consequences. He knows this because you have responded in such a way as to make this true. You must put your attention on how you act, not on how he behaves."

Paz didn't say a word as she raised her head and stared at me. I was silent, but undeterred. Seconds passed before Paz closed her incredulous eyes and dropped her head back to the couch.

"We can only change ourselves, Paz. Sure, he is the bad guy, but you are responsible for your life. Not him. You say you can't leave, but at the same time you don't want to suffer any longer. He drinks. You can't change that. The only thing you can do to make your life with him better is to look at how you have always reacted to him and change it. To keep doing what you have always done, yet expect a different result, is insanity."

Paz opened her eyes and looked at me. "You say I must change?"

"Absolutely, and that is the good news. You have total

control over your own thoughts and actions. This puts you in the driver's seat. The quality of your life won't be dependent on whether or not he is drinking. Since you have decided not to leave him, I can teach you how better to show up for life with a drunk. I can't guarantee happiness, but I can guarantee you will have more self respect."

"Self respect?" Paz sat up.

"Yes, self respect. The first thing you need to do is to stop thinking of yourself as a victim. Then, the second thing is to stop talking to your women friends about how rotten your husband is. This just stirs the pot. You feel depressed and unhappy when you dwell on what all is wrong in your life. You would be better served to start noticing how you react to him. Be an observer of yourself. Write down what you say and do whenever he is drunk. Then we will talk about this and I'll give you suggestions as to how you might change your reaction to him. This is your first assignment, and I'm serious. Most of us go through life with our focus on other people. You need to really get that you are responsible for the quality of your life. Not your husband, but you."

"Now come here." I smiled as I stood up to hug Paz. "You give what I say a try. In a few days I want to hear about your knee jerk reactions to this husband of yours. Then we will see what is to be done with you. Remember now to stop thinking of yourself as a casualty of life. Start paying attention to how you act when he is abusive. Together we will then see what can be done to improve things. It will take time, but time is God's gift."

Little by little I stopped going to church with Sandi.

Tony's thoughts about God and the scheme of things had had more impact on me than I first realized. Tony's scientific leanings made any existence of God an impossibility. He operated on the theory that life is random; you can't prove the claim that we have a soul; one dies and that is the end of it, and there is only the physical world on this planet.

Don't talk to him about aliens or life after death. However, if you did, his logical arguments made sense, especially compared to Michael's constant reference to Spirit as involved with everything from whom to date, to what house to buy, to what job to take. All those years with Michael, I had teased him about using Spirit as a mail-order house and insurance policy.

Then I turned around and let Tony influence me into feeling like there is no God and what comes in life is without meaning. And it didn't help that my life-long inclination had been to doubt there is a loving God who is involved with my life. Without realizing it for a long time, Tony's ideas planted hopelessness in my heart.

I couldn't understand the paradox I had become. On the spiritual level, I longed to make God a part of my life, yet on the mental level I found myself agreeing with Tony. Eventually I noticed my sense of well being diminished with every year I spent in the there-is-no-God box.

Add to that the fact that I had totally misrepresented my sexual history to Tony, and faulted him big time for his. He made the mistake of being honest about his past sex life and what did I do? I judged him as immoral. Me, a prostitute and madam, looked down my nose at a man who had participated in the swinging 70's with his then-wife. I actually felt superior to him. Would that not be the height of hypocrisy?

It ruined our sex life for me. His years of casual, meaningless sex were a turnoff. Did I not remember I had always justified prostitution because sex is a natural bodily function? Now in my senior years I add the morality aspect to it? Not the La Grange fine citizens, but me the reformed prostitute?

As it happened, over time our relationship evolved into a dear, casual, non-sexual one. So as it turned out, both Michael and Tony were men as learning experiences for me. Go figure, but it looked like the passage of time, allowing me to become a student of myself and to put distance from my past, had given me more than I bargained for.

Who I had become begged the questions: Was I redeemed from my past or was I simply now a hypocrite? Was redemption even a possibility? Can a person's past be completely divorced from their present or future? And if so, is that a good thing? The good news was that my past no longer dogged my days. Actually, most days it was hard for me to even remember Miss Edna.

And then one day in the New Mexican Newspaper, there was published evidence that I had lived to make a positive difference in this world of mystery and misdeeds.

"Have you read it yet?" asked Sandi. I could feel her excitement over the phone.

"You bet I have," I smiled and lit yet another Camel.

"The photo of us was really good, too, don't you think?" Sandi said.

"Yes, and I was surprised at the whole presentation. The guy who interviewed us didn't say the article would be a whole page in the Paso Tiempo. I'm feeling plum famous." I laughed and then choked on smoke.

"We will celebrate tonight." Sandi was my social committee.

She continued, "I'll meet you at Rio Chama for wine and eats. All our friends will be there. We can act like celebrities. This is going to be so much fun, and for goodness sakes, dress for the occasion."

I picked up the Friday magazine part of the New Mexican to reread the article entitled, "Retired Teachers Aren't Retired." The human interest article told how Sandi had gone from teaching art at Santa Fe High School to being an art therapist who practiced out of her home studio. And the part about me pointed to how I had spent hours every week volunteering my services as a listener to the troubles of women. Since I wasn't a licensed counselor, my time and thoughts shared with these women were heartfelt, but not professional.

For the first time ever, I loved seeing my name in print. I was proud. Next week I'll mail Della and Jim copies of the article. They will be surprised to hear from me because it isn't Christmas card time.

Epilogue

Months turned into years of retirement and I could feel myself settling into the mystery of it all. I could feel nothing but gratitude in such a wondrous place as Santa Fe. I had friends who loved me; I was safe and secure in my own lovely little home; I had all the money I needed for my life; I was making a contribution to the world by volunteering at the Esperanza Shelter; as yet I didn't have lung cancer from smoking all those Camels, and I had a favorite chaise lounge on my patio for reading and napping. Looking up at the New Mexico blue sky through the tall green trees growing in my yard always soothed my soul.

I was now in the stage of life where not knowing, not totally believing, and not even looking for answers felt best. However, I did have faith that the questions mattered. My senior years were about living the questions without needing answers.

Nap time once again, so as I got comfortable on the lounge, I checked to see if my book and glasses were handy for when I woke up. I was careful to put out my cigarette before giving a last loving look at the bright blue sky.

I always went to asleep easily, but today I was

diverted by memories of the Chicken Ranch, of all things. The recollections were a mix of everything from the commendable to the wretched. Nevertheless, I wasn't distressed by the parade of images from my Texas past. I just let them pass.

Eventually, after a few minutes, I got around to comforting myself with the fact that the Chicken Ranch is a notable piece of Texas history and I was a part of it. And for sure, I've lived gloriously beyond those goddamn days. This was my last thought before finally drifting off to sleep on my patio under the New Mexico sky.

The obituary reported that I died in my sleep. What no one can know is that Ben came for me. He opened the gate. Then slowly, as if in a dream, I moved toward him and into his open arms.

SOURCES

James L. Blaschke, author and historian of the Texas Chicken Ranch.

Michael Brill, numerology chart on Edna Arretha Milton.

Mary Remmers, *Going Down The Line*

John LaFont, *58 Year Around Creede*

Darla J. Blaha, *The La Grange Chicken Ranch Revisited.*

Robbie Davis-Floyd, *Landlady At La Grange: The Folklore of a Texas Madam.*

Al Reinert, "World's Oldest Profession Hits The Road," *Texas Monthly*, 1973.

Saul Friedmon, "The Chicken Ranch," Texas Observer.

Dr. Bernardo Monserrat, retired minister, Center for Spiritual Living, interview.

Maria Pina, *Who Loves Yelapa.*

ABC 13.com, *The Best Little Whorehouse In Texas.*

Dallas Morning News, 8-2-1973, *Chicken Ranch Scratched.*

Fayette County Record, Vol. XXX, Tuesday, 1951.

Wikipedia, *Chicken Ranch (Texas).*

Texas State Archives, *The Sex Salon The Texas Rangers Can't Find.*

News Tempo, June 13, 1955, *Galveston Wide-Open Sin Town.*

ACKNOWLEDGEMENTS

Special Thanks

JUDY ROBINSON, my sister. As my helpful evaluator and analyst, she presided over the fourteen months it took me to write this book. Her enthusiasm for the story kept me at the computer. This collaboration kept us close despite the many miles between Texas and Montana.

JAYME LYNN BLASCHKE, foremost published authority on the Chicken Ranch. It was the chance meeting, when he gave a lecture on the Chicken Ranch at Saint James' Episcopal Church in La Grange, TX, that birthed the idea to make Edna Milton the subject of my next book. Only weeks before, I had moved back to Texas after a twenty-four-year pilgrimage in Arizona, New Mexico, and Mexico. I trusted Jayme's information above all others and he freely shared his research with me.

MICHAEL BRILL, numerologist. Because I wanted to capture the authentic Edna, I enlisted Michael's involvement. Using her full name and birth date, he did the most extensive chart possible. Everything, from her core issue to her greatest strengths and weaknesses of character, was found out. I was careful to keep to the truth of who she was, although some of the places and events are fiction.

MARIA ROCHA, Fayette Heritage Museum and Archives, La Grange, Texas. I lived across the street from the Fayette Public Library, so I walked over many, many times. I was new to the community, and I really appreciated the staff's welcoming and helpful attention. I spent day after day upstairs in the museum with the huge white book that housed the history of the Chicken Ranch. Maria helped me locate and make copies. Then, as a way to get my mind off Edna, I'd check out another movie and head back across Franklin Street for yet another solitary evening in that old green house I loved.

REV. DR. BERNARDO MONSERRAT, Center for Spiritual Living. When I lived in Santa Fe, NM, I attended Bernardo's church. Therefore, when it came time in my novel for Edna to have a spiritual experience, I went to him for assistance. The passage on forgiveness and redemption are his words, verbatim.

ABOUT THE AUTHOR

Joy Jones

Joy Jones, native Texan, returned in 2014 after decades in Arizona and New Mexico to live out her life in the Lone Star State. While living in LaGrange, she attended a lecture on the Chicken Ranch given by Jayme Blaschke. This experience birthed her idea to write a historical fiction based on the life of the last madam of the Chicken Ranch, Edna Milton.

Joy is retired from a career in education. She taught in public schools for over thirty years in Texas and New Mexico. Additionally, she was Student Teacher Coordinator for Northern Arizona University in Flagstaff and she also worked as an Educational Consultant for New Mexico in Santa Fe. She holds a Masters degree in Educational Leadership and a PhD in Transpersonal Psychology.

Joy lives in Galveston, Texas, with her husband, James Nelson. They are relishing their Golden Years together around their nine children and seven grandchildren.

www.ingramcontent.com/pod-product-compliance
Lightning Source LLC
Chambersburg PA
CBHW051641260626
47170CB00004B/1274